THE SAGA OF THE RED BOAR

and other poems

Anthony Weedon

AuthorHouse™ UK Ltd.
500 Avebury Boulevard
Central Milton Keynes, MK9 2BE
www.authorhouse.co.uk
Phone: 08001974150

© 2010 Anthony Weedon. All rights reserved.

No part of this book may be reproduced, stored in a retrieval system, or transmitted by any means without the written permission of the author.

First published by AuthorHouse 5/6/2010

ISBN: 978-1-4490-7601-6 (sc)

This book is printed on acid-free paper.

Writing Poetry

There was once a young girl who came to a great poet and said: 'I wish I could write poetry: I can never get any further than the third line.'

Smiling, the poet replied: 'There's no third line in poetry.'

'Then I'm left with just two.'

'Throw them away.'

'Then I've written nothing.'

'Then you've written poetry.'

'Then poetry is nothing.'

'Poetry is both nothing and everything: it can also be either or neither.'

The girl was enlightened.

DEDICATION

This book of my poems, composed over a number of years, is dedicated to the memory of my late wife Jenny, who was born and brought up as Jennifer Margaret Stow in the small Suffolk village of Waldringfield on the south bank of the tidal estuary of the River Deben in the county of Suffolk. Jenny's father was a schoolmaster whose hobby was building and sailing his own yachts ensuring that Jenny would grow up with a love of sailing and the sea. She was also a strong swimmer and an accomplished rower. But she wasn't interested in competitive sport and games. She simply enjoyed life messing about in boats and keeping as close as possible to nature. She was very good with dogs, cats and other pet animals and loved the wild flowers and birds.

When Jenny was just eleven years old during the severe winter of early 1947, she rode on the ice floes on the River Deben, jumping from one to the other until her concerned father called her to order. This episode epitomised Jenny's attitude to life: it's not there to use us; we're here to use it for the good of all; and Jenny was adept at serving her local community in every possible way. Despite the suffering that life brings to us all, Jenny was always happy and didn't know what it was to be miserable. She was altogether lovely and living with her was an inspiration. She encouraged me to write and enjoyed reading everything I wrote. This book is dedicated to her memory. I would like to record my appreciation of the help and encouragement afforded me by Carol Walmsley, Rosemary Williams, Maureen Rankin and Jean Vernon in the production of this work.

Anthony Weedon

INTRODUCTION

The Saga of the Red Boar is a creation myth in which the universe is personified as a mother goddess in the shape of a great sow with galaxies of offspring. Our own sun is envisaged as White Boar, whose son in the shape of Red Boar creates life upon planet earth, sacrificing his own life in the process. Eons later Red Boar resurrects in an attempt to teach Man to live in harmony with nature. Man seems to heed Red Boar whose teaching is soon lost. Rediscovered recently as global warming begins to take effect, Red Boar's message again shows Man what must be done to save the planet.

The theme of our relationship with the natural world is a thread running through all the poems following on from the Saga and the essence of art is seen as a means by which we express this relationship. Sometimes art is personified in the shape of a great horse known as Art Horse who sees true art as the champion of harmonious existence within the web of life. Other animals also appear in the poems, in particular the wolf known as Winter Waster, who is seen as man's alter ego epitomising his better nature. Goddess, woman, wolf, boar, horse, crow, raven, rook are all pictured as forces for good whilst gods, man, doves and pigeons are seen as the real badies.

The collection also includes four short stories in the form of folk tales expressing how true happiness is a product of both our living in harmony with the natural world around us on the one hand and of nature-inspired artistic expression on the other. Humour and realism are inter-twined to insure an enjoyable read. A section of the poems under the heading LIGHT VERSE AND WORSE are full of rollicking fun based on the East Anglian humour remembered from my Suffolk childhood, which strongly influences everything I write.

Some of the poems, too numerous to list here, have appeared in various periodicals and anthologies and some of them have won prizes in competitions. However, since readers will make their own choice as to which poems they like best, I prefer not to single out any poem for special mention here.

Anthony Weedon

THE GREAT SOW

The universe is.
Abides, an infinite sow;
Lives, a great black sow;
Sustains; her offspring numberless.

Erupting from her womb,
This churning mass squeals,
Struggling to be fed from fiery milk.
See how it turns some into burning boars!
See how they pull their chariots in arcs
To intersect across her seething bulk!

Some die, are trampled down;
Some fall, or so it seems, deep down.
Such are devoured within their mother's bulk,
But not destroyed.
Recycling them, she twirls more boars into the void;
Her womb is never closed;
She flows through all.

Death's missiles come and go.
She fends them off with never tiring snout,
Refusing to release the unreturnable,
Or to define redemption for the few.

The depth of her indifference augurs deep,
Matched only by her never ending care.
Here is her essence and her unity,
Diffusion more decisive than her stars
Milk-massed in swirling herds of hurtling boars.

Made she never was,
Nor shall she ever be destroyed.
Living, she falls, dies, rises,
Giving again her life from the timeless cinders,
Heaving all into nothingness,
Only to return again
To fill the void with rejoicing.

Bringing peace through toiling coils of pain,
In grunting harmony she hymns her tune,
Telling out to every listening ear her endless song:

Creation never was:
All that is depends on all that was;
And was is IS;
And IS is infinite.

THE BIRTH OF RED BOAR

White Boar: burnished bright
And master moulded;
Conceived in turmoil;
Furnace formed in the womb's fire,
Body-shaped in the Great Sow.

Sharp tusks gleaming bright,
His inner power flaming hot,
He races onward,
Ever onward, into the void
Hauling his dark chariot.

Shedding beams of light,
Piercing solid nothingness,
Spreading creation,
White Boar spins, sprinkling his blood
In twirling balls of red fire.

Tusk cut traces snap;
The chariot, Doom Killer,
Shatters night-like gloom,
Her molten, slashing wheel knives
Swinge-crashing through black space holes.

Hounded by ice-fangs,
Spluttering, Doom Killer cools
And circles White Boar
Like a crusty old cinder,
Hole-blasted but undaunted.

Pink Snout, Boar's artist,
Sniffs at cooling Doom Killer,
And, tossing her round,
Twirls her faster and faster,
Forming a ball, smooth and brown.

Then, as White Boar spins,
His right eye twists and drops out
Under his trotter,
Where it turns into Red Boar,
Creator and Life Giver.

RED BOAR CREATES LIFE

Squealing in fury,
White Boar seized tiny Red Boar
In his foaming jaws
And threw him, screaming, earthwards
And downwards onto the Brown Ball.

Ripping and rooting,
Red Boar charged over the smooth surface,
Heaping up mountains,
Digging out the ocean beds,
Breathing to create the air.

Snorting out wet breath,
He created the rain clouds;
Rising, they became a canopy
Covering the brown earth ball.
His beating heart became time;
His red bristles became the lightning;
His grunts became the thunder;
His hot blood flowed, scouring out the river beds;
The rain running along them filled the sea beds;
His urine salted the seas;
The froth from his jaws became wave-leaping white horses;
His ears became the folds in the ground;
His flicking tongue imbued both land and sea with colour;
His sperm fused with his brain cells,
Forming the essence of life;
His tough snout became desire;
His trotters turned into suffering;

He flicked his curly tail, creating beauty;
His eyes became windows into the All-Mind;
So Red Boar created life.

And his bones became Death.

Sun-bleached and tide-washed,
His carcase lay, sand polished:
Aeons passed away:
Life progressed and multiplied,
Living, crying and dying.

Down the long ages
Nothing touched the sacred bones,
The sacred bones of the Life-Giver,
The Lord of Life, the Red Boar,
The Essence of Life.
Nothing touched the bones;
Nothing save the elements:
The sand, the tides, the wind and the sun,
Especially the sun,
The soul of White Boar, the parent of Red Boar,
Red Boar, the ray of the sun's heart.

Watching over his son,
White Boar, through time,
Sent him several visitors:
Eight noble visitors came to view the bones of Red Boar,
Eight noble life forms;
Eight forms stemming from the boar-essence;
Eight in the beating time of Boar's heart;
Eight within time;
Eight without time;
Eight came there,
Eight.

ALBATROSS VISITS THE BONES

Across the cloud-hugged seas soared Albatross,
There high, here low to clip the crested waves
That rise like Pegasus to challenge him;
But, driven by the ceaseless westerlies,
They sweep before him, longing for the sun.
Undaunted still, he planes his endless way,
This girdler of the globe and wanderer,
All-Seer of the shades of things to come.

Ahead a sandy shore came into view,
As breaking clouds at last released the sun
To burn its way across the rolling sands,
Revealing, far below, the bones of Boar.

Unmelted here upon this southern shore,
Remaining here despite the blazing sun,
This is a heap of snow, thought Albatross.
And told this story round the seven seas
Then, flying lower, nearer to the bones,
He made them out to be white seals asleep
And told the world how he had never seen
So many of them resting in one place.

Then, once again, he flew in nearer still,
And this time thought he recognised his own,
A group of albatrosses standing there,
Not knowing how to leave the sands behind
For want of thermal currents in the air.
Now, puzzled, did he steer as near he dare,
And recognised, at last, the bones of Boar.

Then, angry clouds blown from the boiling west,
Came bringing hail and whipped him round about,
And drove him far across the raging seas,
This girdler of the globe and wanderer,
Who fled distraught to tell the world the truth,
And has so done and does until this day,
Of how he'd seen a god upon the shore.

KESTREL VISITS THE BONES

Kestrel hovering above the bones
Saw no use at all in them for her:
Far too low to form a useful perch;
Far too open for a hidden nest;
Far too scattered for a sheltered hide;
Far too old to hold a scrap of meat;
Thus she saw them till she thought again.

Then she thought how useful they could be:
In their shadow many mice could mate;
In their crannies they could build their nests,
Underneath them find some juicy slugs;
Beetles too; and all to plump them up,
Morsels, grey and sleek with tenderness,
Growing fat for her to kill and eat.

Thinking on, she saw their ugliness:
Faceless, worm infested, staring skull;
Beetle-bared and rifled, scattered bones,
Charnel, splintered by the jackal's jaws;
Once imbued with sickly-sweet decay;
Fly-tormented, torn by beak and claw;
Now a wasted heap of gutlessness.

The beauty of the bones then shone and spoke,
As, fashioned with much care and temple-like,
This frame of joy and hold of graceful power,
Reflected back resource towards the sun,
As hidden tissues waited to be turned
Along a patterned labyrinth of paths
To raise the mind once more to mindfulness.

ROOK VISITS THE BONES

Then came there Rook.
Come quick! He said,
Come quick and look;
A great ox dead!
Come bird and beast
And make a feast.
Insects, grubs, maggots,
Bone-marrow, faggots,
All kinds of tasty food and treats galore:
A carcase lying here upon the shore!

Then came they all flying,
Singing and sighing,
Running and skipping'
Leaping and tripping,
Trotting and tramping,
Stumbling and stamping,
Fussing and flopping,
Jumping and hopping,
To see for themselves.

Rook with his rooklings
Flew to the food fields,
Found there the best food,
Capered and feasted,
Laughed as he ate it,
This cheater of creatures
And arch-crook of cheaters.

Cheated and angry,
The animals cursed rook;
Harried and chased him
Home from the food fields,
Beat him and raced him
And called him a black crook.

Then came rook's mate:
Come soon! She said,
Come soon, not late!
A sheep lies dead;
Come see its fleece
Without a crease:
Linings for your nests galore
Lying there upon the shore!

Then came they all flying,
Singing and sighing,
Running and skipping'
Leaping and tripping,
Trotting and tramping,
Stumbling and stamping,
Fussing and flopping,
Jumping and hopping,
To see for themselves.

Then wise Missus Rook
Went flying to look
For all the best sites
For her and her friend rooks,
To use for their nest sites
In treetops and branch crooks.

Fuming and flustered,
The birds came and cursed Rook,
And built in the hedgerows,
Nesting in any nook,
Even in burrows,
And when these were taken,
Laid eggs in the furrows.

Then came Child Rook:
Come now! He said,
Come now and look!
A whale lies dead
Within your reach
Upon the beach:
A mighty bone house lying there upon the shore
Providing shelter from the storm for birds and more!

Then came they all flying,
Singing and sighing,
Running and skipping'
Leaping and tripping,
Trotting and tramping,
Stumbling and stamping,
Fussing and flopping,
Jumping and hopping,
To see for themselves.

Then flew those bad rooks,
Laughing and jesting,
Out to the best roosts
For the night's resting.

Then all the animals were flaming furious,
And cursed themselves for having been so curious;
They went and asked the owl to take his wisdom book
Along to have a quiet word with Mister Rook.

Said Owl to Rook: You seem to be a clever bird;
But how to use your talents well you've never heard:
The purpose of sound speech is to communicate,
But you have used its powers to lie and dominate.

Not so! Said Rook; and, look you here, I tell you true
Of when you can expect the storms to come and go;
But, choosing not to notice when I tell them right,
The other birds complain when clouds come into sight.

Now, having listened to their silly chitter-chat,
You fly in here and talk to me of this and that;
If they don't like it now because I've told them lies,
I'll happily desist from giving warning cries.

No, please, I beg of you, continue giving these,
Said Owl as flustered as a breeze among the trees.
You have no need to feel you're just a buffer bird;
Without your forecasts all of us would suffer hard:
So please feel free to tell us what you see and hear
Of signs that point to what the coming day will bear.
So now when rooks churn overhead and have their say,
You can be sure a storm is not so far away.

THE WOLVES VISIT THE BONES

Wolf Prelude

Petals blowing from the remnant dawn,
Silver cirrus sun-stained in the dusk,
Speeding out across the twilight gap,
Pierce the darkling doors of closing night.

Curling petals, shot-hued by the sun,
Peeling upward on the western wind,
Driving grooves of hope through dusky skies,
Tell the coming of tomorrow's dawn.

Swirling petals, curving passed the stars,
Turning grey like wisps of waving hair,
Fleeing fast before the waxing wind,
Herald now the coming of the wolves.

Advent of the Wolves

Petalled pink upon their panting tongues,
The Wolves bay fealty to the storm-sped moon,
As, bounding through the marrams in the dunes,
They reach the lapping margins of the tide.

Led by Winter Waster, Lord of Wolves,
They pause beside the bleaching bones of Boar,
Beside the ceaseless sea's incessant lash,
To sniff out wisdom from the passing years.

Smiling pink, the wise old wolf lord spook:
Here lie the bones that taught the world to be,
That taught the wolf pack how to live and act,
And showed it how to share and made it free.

SEAGULL VISITS THE BONES

Raucous refuse house,
Engulfer of the sea's disturbed malevolence,
Sits sentinel, a mobile trash can,
Waiting on the empty skulls of yearless yesterdays,
Guarding fearful doubts and
Holding them in place
Across the knees of cultivating apes
To tremble them before
The fertile fields of their defiance.

When Seagull landed beside the bones
He was no longer interested.
Having seen them so many times before,
He wondered what all the fuss was about.
Billing around for morsels, he wasn't pleased
When all he found was an inedible shoe and an old sock.
He preferred shoes to be filled with maggots,
But this one wasn't. All it had was some crawling thing
Ensconced inside its toe, out of reach
And infuriating. Just like life in general:
Never any good unless there was something to complain about,
And squabble over like the dead guts of a pig,
Always good for a tug o' war on a rubbish tip.
Here it was different; these bones weren't even refuse;
They had been here far too long for that.

Then he became thoroughly disgusted with himself
For allowing himself to be led into a train of thought,
Especially about these more than dead,
And passed being trash,
Bones belonging to some nonentity,
Whose guts must surely have entertained seagulls
In some far distant and long forgotten age.
Ah well, who was he to set himself up as a judge?
If that were indeed so,
Then perhaps the old bones were worth
A nod of the head after all.
So that's what he did:
Nodded to them and flew away.

SEAGULL VISITS THE BONES
(continued)

The One-Eyed Duck

Blackthorn bushes bathed in shade
The deep end's dominance
Beside the duck pond's denigrating depths,
When, blown from the ashen skies upon the East Wind's back,
This Seagull lit despondent
Seeking sanctuary within the temple of the dark pond's lure,
Remembering the times he'd perched upon the skulls
To meditate about his livelihood.

Suddenly, as shrieked the East Wind's piercing voice,
Wintering the early spring with icy tears,
Seagull perceived a sudden, flashing white ebullience
Of blackthorn blossom
Bursting through the dull, despairing gloom.

Wreathed in this ephemeral brilliance
A one eyed duck peeped
From the thicket of the blackthorn's universe
As one who staggers, mangle-minded,
From a truth filled cavern
To briefly glimpse a half-truth
Before it fades beyond the rim of fond desire.

Feathered in the self-sufficient fortress of his frame,
The floating gull saw then and knew
The answer to despondency, the child of fond desire:
He would scavenge on the refuse path
A sunlit way of peace through dying life
To build afresh the force of living death,
To blaze the bursting joy of blackthorn blooms
To all the universe.

Seagull saw sweet joy across the bones

Then once in aeons moved the skull of Boar:
Moved once and then returned to stillness
On the sands in waiting,
Waiting silently the seventh and the eighth,
Waiting for the last two visitors,
Waiting for their advent on the sands,
Waiting patiently his own return.

ELEPHANT VISITS THE BONES

Rolling along to the great waves beat,
Elephant ambled on cushioned feet;
Strolling along by the ebbing tide,
He squirted sea on his folding hide.

Effortless, effortless was his gait,
He waved his trunk at a gentle rate;
His huge ears flapped on his nodding head;
He shouted loud and the seabirds fled.

Stomping along on the shelving shore,
He saw on the sands the bones of Boar;
He pushed and shoved at their chalk-white mass;
But, strive as he might, they would not pass.

Twisting his trunk round the heap, he tugged,
And pressed his tusks and heaved and hugged,
Holding it close like the sea's firm grip,
The grip it has on a sinking ship.

In this trial of strength the great beast learnt,
His efforts wasted, his substance burnt,
How futile it was to fight the rhyme
Of the tide's debate with timeless time.

SANDPIPER VISITS THE BONES

Sandpiper's line was aimless purpose
The world fell away before him
It seeped away at his feet
The waste seemed endless
They made him President
He presided over a bankrupt currency
He ignored heaps of bones
He played around piles of refuse
Allowing them to remain
He pursued the disintegration
He was undeterred by the holocaust
He pried into everyone's affairs
Without causing a disturbance
There was employment for everyone
Sandpiper never misinterpreted
He bobbed up and down on a rock
Observing disintegration and wasteful seepage
With concentrated indifference
He awaited the washing out of everything
With unperturbed non-involvement
Allowing for the nefarious purpose of the takeover
As chaos became the concentration
Of his aimless purpose
And nobody was employed anymore
As he bobbed through the swoosh of his need
In an unendeavour to know anything
Until the aim of his purpose
Became his desireless disinterest
And he abdicated beside the rushing sea.

MAN VISITS THE BONES

Mind Emergence

Cliffs fortify Man;
Roots force his empty skull holes;
His mind without him,
He skulks amongst cringing rocks;
Sand scours stones into bannocks.

The sea washes the black rocks;
Man watches the sea;
His mind dances out beyond its farthest reach;
It folds, mobile in its hide,
The rhythms of the earth.

The dome of the greatest skull is blue;
Marram roots bind the sandpits;
Mind seeks to bind grass to the sunrise
To float them as one over the sea,
As the blood of Man infuses the seascape.

The sea's amoebic fingers
Slip the sliding sand;
Gripless, they belie the fisted waves,
Which punch the stone-born bannocks
Far into the shelving rocks.

Spattering the dancing mind with thoughts,
The bannocks chit and chatter,
Plummeting to bounce the blue skies hollow song
Across the rooting grasses,
Binding fast the blood's escaping power.

Man Investigates

Man leaps from the rocks;
With his antler pick he digs the cliff for flints;
Resting, he observes the merging shore
Snaking northwards to where the cliffs disperse,
Giving place to shoals of swirling sand.

His feet sponged by the soft sand,
He walks by the sea,
Observing sun-blinded bones:
He comes upon a white-ribbed castle
Wardened by a tusked and grinning skull.

Overawed, he lauds the shining bones;
Its teeth are no portcullis
To his lithographic mind.
He priests the warden,
Temples out the ribs;
Raw, he worships, wondering the way of bones;
Mindfully, he clothes the skull in flesh.

Forest pigs invade his striving mind;
Leaping from the temple to the sands,
He drums a ritualistic beat,

Working with his feet
Magic missiles for the pigs;
Working with his mind
To use the bones as weapons,
Clubbing down the fleeing swine
Already weakened
By a hail of javelins.

Dashing in a frantic, frenzied run,
He grasps a fallen femur
Lying by the ribs:
Still it lies unbudged by all his tugs:
Rushing back inside the ribs, he sweats.

The bones form his home
Whilst he seeks out his purpose,
Timing his breathing
Through the thought of their being
Best stolen for his dwelling.
Bones are flower patterns
Controlling delusiveness:
Charm setters, binding
Man in his fluctuations
In the bower of thoughtfulness.

Bones are beautiful,
Determining femininity
And fertile:
Man seeks to flint-carve charmlets:
The sharp edge refuses to mark them.
Bones pattern the sand;

Shall they tell tomorrow's dawn?
They draw no pictures;
Tomorrow's dawn never comes;
Yesterday is the future.

Man becomes disturbed,
Desiring the yesterdays,
Seeking the future,
Seeking magic in the bones,
Making them blinded liars,
Unheeding their miracle.

They madden his mind;
He desires to powder them,
Drinking their essence
To caper in ecstasy,
Dancing down the tumbling cliffs.

Tripping and tramping,
Man yells defiance;
Hopping and stamping,
Dances the bone dance,
Rolling to ox-horn,
Leaping to horse-prance
Waving to green corn,
Twirling to bowstring,
Stamping with bare feet,
Shaking when birds sing;
Bladder is drum beat;
Man skips the bone ring.
Peace is the wave beat:

Man perceives through the sea spray
Pearly white boar tusks;
Stopping, he kneels down,
Kneels by the boar skull,
And fondles their tenderness,
So smooth and silky:
Slashing great boar tusks,
Sharp as a flint edge.

Using his flint knife,
Carving, he whittles,
Whittles a top tusk;
Carves out a small pig,
Just as he's seen one
Under the oak trees.

Fingers fondle the tusk pig,
Merging its inscape with exploring sea spray:
Man's reflecting poignancy,
Pricking his breath into ivory,
Breathes his power through plasmic certitude.

Burping bubbles mock the sea's retreat:
Angrily it arches back
Clawing out for fresh purchase;
Reaching and whacking at the boar bones,
It beetles out the sand beneath the gargoyled skull,
Moving out in seconds what
Eons long ineptitudes had failed to do.

Clutching at the sand eddies, the skull totters,

And topples into the beetled pit;
Prowling bubbles gurgitate the sand,
Sucking down the fallen temple priest;
The temple disintegrates;
Man flees the devastation;
As thrown by a wave,
He slaps, face down, upon the sand.

His fingers tell of tournures
Turning in the compass of his palm:
He sets the susine effigy among the marrams;
Chanting, he kneels and breathes magic,
Worshipping eye-blinking whiteness under the sun-glare.

The Spell

Bubble, bubble, breathe the spray,
Double, double, through the day;
Take a pinch of Albatross,
In the plasma let it toss:
Double, double, dig the sand,
Shake the rubble on the land:
Rip the riding Kestrel's eye,
Rise the West Wind's soothing sigh;
Tasking, hurry up the deed,
Boil Windhover's eye for seed:
Stand and let the Black Rook speak,
Let him stir it with his beak;
Throwing in the Wolf King's howl,
Stir it well within the bowl:
Bubble, bubble, breathe the spray,
Breathe the blood of earth today:
Take the Mammoth's curly tusk,
Grind it up from dawn to dusk;
Throw it in and stir it round,
Dance his cushions on the ground:
Slither in the Seagull's joy,
Let his laughter serve this ploy;
Let Sandpiper not preside
Lest his negligence deride:
Take and use what he shall find,
Throw it in and let it bind:
Bubble, bubble, breathe the spray,
Breathe its power throughout the day.

Man himself shall know what's good,
Cut himself and use the blood;
Press it where the wound is sore,
Press it on the little boar;
Let it redden out his hide,
Stand him there in all his pride;
He has seen the Dance of Eight,
Now he need no longer wait:
Deeply, deeply, take this breath,
Life shall take the place of death!

THE REBIRTH OF RED BOAR

The tusk pig shuddered,
Broadening his boarders, breathing air.
He breathed the tangy turmoil of ten thousand seas:
He breathed the milling cries of birds innumerable:
He breathed the mingled scent of countless flowers:
He breathed the agony of death's putrescence:
He breathed the penetrating scent of swine
Rooting forest mould for sustenance.
He breathed the mistful divot's mystic odour:
He breathed the body mist of Mother Goddess:
Redolent with all her mindfulness.
Recreated now upon the dunes,
He breathed the essence of his own creation,
Growing once again into Red Boar.

Over-uttered by the buzz of flies,
Man gasped and knelt amongst the marram grass.
Tool-less now, no dancer anymore,
Man, this man, was the one who saw
Beauty in the curling tail of Boar,
Beauty in his shoulder, snout and tusk;
Saw him as the darling of his soul,
Saw him now as none had ever seen,
Learnt from him the truth that none had known,
Leant from him enough to stop the rot,
Learnt from him before it was too late,
Learnt to be the master of his fate.

BOAR TEACHES MAN

The tail of the Great Boar curled
Beside a fly on a stalk of marram grass,
Growing from the swirling sand,
Growing from the wheezing tunes
Played by breezes following the sea's recoil.

He turned to look overland,
Over the marshland,
Over the undulations,
Over the play of its green couture
Waving a reed dance in time to the sand tunes.

Then, looking at Man, he said:
Do not worship me;
Sit upon my back;
Come with me along the Path;
Ride with me over the marsh.

Holding the bog path, Boar stole through the reed beds,
Moulding the sunlight in blues, greens and bright reds,
Kingfishers darted from alders to moss banks:
Rings of bright water dispersed through the reed banks.

Grasshopper warblers were churning their chain song;
Brassy brown bitterns were beating their boom gong;
Swooping blue swallows were mawing up midges,
Stooping green willows were sweeping the ridges.

Hawking grey harriers hunted the brown hare;
Stalking black bulrushes reached for the fresh air;
Otters were searching for eels in the bog holes;
Trotters of Red Boar were squelching passed field voles.

Careless of gnat bites, unheeding their itch-pain,
Bare legs by nettles stung, man gripped the boar mane.
Draining the water, this marsh shall be my land;
Gaining this rush bowl, I'll here make my own stand.

No, said the wise Boar, that way spells disaster;
Follow the pathway and learn to be master:
Make up your mind to dispose of the old day;
Take a firm hold and I'll teach you the true way.

STRANGER IN THE VALLEY

An industrious people once lived
Folded in the bowl of a broad vale
Surrounded by long-topped downs
Rolling far away into the outlands.
This bowl was the only world they knew:
It was the path of their existence;
So they tended it carefully.

Down from the East Downs
Over the meadows
On a grey charger came riding so softly
Into the valley came riding this stranger
Clothed in find purple and blond as the sunlight
Over the meadows
He rode by the streamside
Over the meadows
Looking at wild flowers
Down by the river he watered his tired horse,
Down by the river dismounting he drank there,
Seeing the mauve flowers
Over the meadows.
There came a tired housewife
Over the meadows
To wash by the streamside the clothes of her man.
Smiling politely, the stranger addressed her:
This water's the best I've tasted this year.
Sorely the woman complained of its hardness.
We long for some rain in our eave butts, she said.
It wearies me traipsing on

Over the meadows;
My feet are so sore I wish they were gone.

Leading his horse, the stranger proceeded
On to the township to lodge for the night.

At the inn he met a hulking fellow:
Redpate Pete who wore a shirt of yellow,
And never knew that shirts were washed by dames
In hardened water whilst he played at games.
Not showing his surprise, the stranger said:
Across the Western Downs I saw a head:
At least, a hill appeared to be so shaped.
Redpate, surprised, oped up his mouth and gaped.
None here, he said, has ever seen this sight.
Are you certain that you've seen aright?
You can best see it coming from the East;
Once down within the vale the picture ceased.
The stranger said. But then I saw a sight
That made me want to sing out in delight:
Growing in profusion, rare mauve flowers,
For which, in other places, men search hours.
Good gracious! Redpate said, they must have need;
For here along this valley they're a weed!
Good stranger, I've lived here all my days,
And thought I knew the valley and its ways;
But you've seen things I've never seen before,
Even though you've only passed the door.
The stranger smiled; he used the utmost tact;
In life, good Redpate, I've learnt this fact:
That he who follows well along the Way
Learns more than he who tends it day by day.

Out on the morrow
The stranger went riding
Over the meadows
Away to the West,
Over the meadows,
Away to the Outlands
Never again to return to the valley,
Never again to stay at the inn.

Redpate, however,
Yes, Redpate remembered
Remembered and tried hard to follow the Way.
Over the meadows
He walked in the evenings;
Over the meadows
He walked in the day.

He who is walking across the green meadow
Learns more than the grubber whose eyes are cast low.

Man was pleased.
He enjoyed the story about the stranger,
About the valley and the meadows.
Tell me more, he said.
Red Boar, I like your stories.

BONE STORY

Here's a story about my bones, said Boar

Albatross saw them;
Kestrel discerned them;
Rook played the fool with them;
Wolf failed to gnaw them;
Elephant could not move them;
Seagull saw the joy in them;
Sandpiper ignored them;
Man sought to use them;
The Bones of Boar denied him,
And taught him to know them.

Teach me more, Red Boar,
Teach me more:
Who am I?
What am I?
Where am I going?

You are Man, this man;
This man is an epitome of Man;
He's the age of Man in every age.
Red Boar is Boar, the beauty of the earth,
The ageless essence of the blue sky's worth.

Rising like the rim of a saucer,
The edge of the marsh bordered man's mind.
What do we find when we reach the edge? He asked.
There's always the Beyond, replied Red Boar;

The well trodden path maintains itself;
The Path obliterates the way of the man;
Who stops to tend a section of it.
Whatever the situation, there's always the distance;
Before the beginning there's always that which begat it.
After the end there's always the sequel;
Though you travel at the speed of light,
There's always the horizon;
Numbers are endless, horizon limitless.
Time is an unsurfaced line
Bisecting the photonic curve of a universe.
The line in the curve is now;
Path and goal are now;
You and I are now;
The marsh, the heat and the flies are now.
The path leads through the All-Mind;
Now is the All-Mind.

Is progress not good?
Surely there's a better way to cut than with flaked flints?

Effectiveness is not to be confused with progress.
Whatever you discover,
Whatever you find along the Path,
Use that as an aid to walk the Path.
He who uses discoveries to widen the Path
Misuses his advantage,
Losing himself in a labyrinth,
Where he begins to see change as progress,
And thinks he stands on the horizon.
Glibly he talks of big bangs and origins,

Age and expansions,
And continues looking for the edge of all things,
As he allows Mind to disintegrate,
And dissipate itself into individual nonentities.

Fingers point the Way;
Face up to reality;
See change in the permanent factor
And abide in the eternal now.

MARSH HYMN

The marsh shouted to the sky:
Pan your music into my saucer,
Chatter my echo into the clouds,
Clothe my nights in dew,
My mornings in mistfulness;
Sorrow is in my stillness;
Laughter is in my silence;
There's no end to my industry.

The sky was all smile;
It smiled on the marsh and said:
Play your reed pipes in the wind;
Kiss my skirts with the dew of your peace;
All is one under my canopy;
Your industry shall be rewarded;
Tears and laughter shall rain upon you.

The Journey Continues

When they reached the edge of the marsh Man became sad;
He was glad to rest under an oak tree.
In the confusion of his feelings
He composed a little song,
Which he sang to Boar like this:

When the sun shines bright and all is well
How I wish the clouds would break the spell:
How I wish that they would come and stand
Shielding my feet from this burning sand.
When the clouds are thick and black as night
How I wish for just one ray of light;
How I wish the sun would pierce the gloom
When I sit forlorn within my room.

Sun without clouds and nothing will grow;
Joy without sorrow, no one can know:
But what is sorrow and what is joy?
Which will support us and which will cloy?

Boar was pleased.
There's truth in what you sing, he said.
There's a saying:
He who rests too soon, rests for too long.
And don't forget:
This man is the age of Man in every age.

Red Boar didn't tire at all;
He didn't tire of teaching this man;
This man would soon become Man,
Who would become numerous;

Too numerous for Boar to teach;
Today he must teach this man
That all be not lost before this man should know the truth.
That's why he told the tale of Man Failure.

MAN FAILURE

Man was primitive.
Red Boar talked to him.
Man became depressed.
Boar sang to the stars.
Man was elated.
Boar rooted the earth.
Man philosophised.
Boar flipped him over.
Man cultivated the earth.
Boar assisted him.
Man soon became sophisticated.
Boar soon became primitive.
Man enjoyed being a sardine.
Boar smelt the sardines.
Man wept in his sardine tin.
Boar crushed the empty tin in his jaws.

SONG OF SHULVER

On his hindquarters,
Under the oak tree,
Red Boar sat
And taught man,
Saying

In the field this young man ploughed.
Two horses teamed, manes tossing,
Pulled, earth-slicing through his dreams,
The moulding plough, manipulating,
Through imprisoning traces,
Flicking ears, anticipating flies'
Desire for bloody orgies.

Three things remember:
So his peasant father said:
There's no hurry;
For you've two weeks to plough this field.
Observe the ways of life around you;
Be considerate to your plough team.

The young man grew impatient.
What nonsense!
I can plough this field in half the time.
What a bore it is
To have to watch the same old trees and places
Day by day!
These horses are well fed and watered,
Resting through the night.
What further considerations do they need?

As he ploughed
He came across three girls
Each standing at a point,
Selected by herself,
Along a boundary line
On headlands hedgerow-bound by heaving hawthorn,
Old man's beard and bryony.
Each girl communicated with him,
Each with her particular face and posture,
With glance and gesture,
With clothes worn clearly,
With words melodiously spoken,
With seducing smiles,
Reaching for miles
Beyond the searching arrows of disaster.

There was this girl sat sleek,
Black-haired and impish,
Cross-legged and pinafored,
Black skirt short above her knees
Magpied by her white blouse:
Dark eye depths discerning the soul of white:
Short hair revealing
Brash white teeth between blood red lips
That crimsoned out all life in one brief gush.

Nerina was her name,
She tended sheep,
And danced the sheep shorn pastures,
Moulding with her flock the rolling knolls:
Observers of the brown arena,
Where striving menfolk spurted youth,
Slanting their observations upward
From the ploughland's virile flow.
Nerina named the young man Shulver.
Leaping up, she skipped.
Her buttocks quivered
As she flipped her leg from pointed knee,
Twirling on tiptoe, calling:
Shulver come and play with me!

Shulver's second day was wearisome.
Tinder taut, his mind snapped sharp,
Seeking to spark his liquid legs,
Fatigued by driving hard his horses,
Tired by having ploughed too much the day before.

Seeing Nerina seated, he desired her;
When she danced he longed for her the more,
Longed to free himself from weary toil,
Longed to skip in freedom round the knolls.
Turning on the headland, he looked up,
Sensed and saw her dancing through the sheep.
Many deny the voice of sounds they hear,
Giving them no music, message, warning or delight.
Other ears were deaf to sounds Nerina heard:
Breeze blustered undulations,

Caught by leaves, musicked her hands.
Causing them to weave mosaic rhymes;
Whistling curlews threw her legs in twirls;
Bumble bees beat rhythms for her feet;
Grass, fleece-flounced, played tunes for flickered lids,
Semaphoring sparkles to the lark from flashing eyes.

Beating, bending, bowing, leaping high,
Nerina bounded, laughing on the lea:
Shulver, hurry, come and play with me!

Inattentive, longing to be free,
Voiceless sounds were all that Shulver heard.
Left unattended, waiting worn and tired, his horses stood.
Scrambling through the hedge he stretched his arms,
Reaching out to join Nerina's play.
Slugs slime stones more gracefully than he could dance:
Tussock-tripped, he fell full length upon the turf:
Laughing loud, Nerina skipped her mirth:
You're too tired to play with me, she said.

Raging, Shulver laid his impotence upon the sod:
The thought that even powerful spurts
Sometimes fall short of their intended target
Brought no comfort.
So he resolved, in peasant pride, to plough more stately,
Manfully denying dark Nerina's power.

Shulver, ploughing on the following day,
Came near to where the second girl sat fey.

Here was a floppy-hatted goldilocks,
Seated, clasping knees, full-flounced and frilly-frocked,
Her blue eyes peering through a haze of tumbling hair
Clouding like mists on meadows
Yellow-clothed in buttercups
Concealing buds rose-tipped far rosier
Than rose bay willow herb.
Brichtina her name,
Her clothes belied her life
Led in the town amidst the flashing lights.
Sirenaciously she sang softly
As she stood
Inviting contact:

When the toil bugs hurt
And you're tired of work,
Come along with me
To the town so free,
To the corner dive,
Where the world's alive:
To the busy street,
Where people meet:
Relax yourself there
In a metal chair,
As you sip your beer
With men of good cheer.
Come along with me
To the town so free,
When the toil bugs hurt
And you're tired of work:
Come out of the storm

From the cloud's black form:
Come in from the rain
To the place of gain:
Come into the town
Where cash is paid down:
You'll not be alone
When your work is done:
Come walking with me
In the streets so free;
I'll show you the sights
'Neath the city lights,
When the toil bugs hurt,
And you're tired of work.

Having hastily unhitched his team,
Shulver hurried home.
Smilingly his father answered his request to work in town.
Mist does not deter a dissatisfied man;
Only sunshine will enlighten him.
Go, my son, learn truth,
Remembering, however, always that
No one else may plough where you have ploughed.

Father, surely 'tis better
That I perish in the mists,
Floundered by my own ineptitude,
Than that I should stagnate
Beneath your well intentioned care?
So he took his leave and went to town,
Where, one day, he would become a clown.

Brichtina thought that he should have a bash

At working for the council, who paid cash.
So, issued with a broom and small dust cart,
At cleaning up the streets he made a start.
Empty beer cans, tins of metal polish,
Twisted spoons, he swept them all with relish:
Shovelling all, he filled his cart with muck.
At certain times there came a large dust truck,
Which, with a metal arm, his small cart gripped,
Lifted high and all its contents tipped
Into its rear end where it squashed them down,
Churned them up and moved on round the town.

One day a storm arose, a black cloud burst;
Shulver sheltered, but he never cursed.
Music sounded through the pouring rain;
It was the water gurgling down a drain:
Brightly coloured beer cans floated by,
Red, gold and green, their beauty made him sigh.
He thought the city was a lovely place.
He found Brichtina had much more than face,
Especially at night within her flat,
Where it can be guessed what they were at.
She, however, soon began to nag,
Complaining always of an empty bag.
The bubbling drains, even the beer cans, palled;
And even when the rumbling dust cart called
To lift his little cart into the air,
He gazed into the sky and felt despair.
Perfumed breezes blew across the town
From off the hills and he felt like a clown
Performing in a circus ring for drips,

Whose lives were naught but beer, hard work and trips.
He left his cart and went back to the farm
Where in a field the third girl sought to charm.
Brenda, her name, she wore a yellow blouse;
Her overall dark brown, she milked the cows.

Observing all about him carefully,
The chastened Shulver ploughed more steady now,
As, caring for the welfare of his team,
He sniffed the healing scent of fresh turned earth,
And savoured it above the slicing sound
Of share and scrape of breast against the stones,
Whilst seagulls came, ballooning in his wake,
Like one vast mass of white integrity,
To cry their overtones to plodding hooves
Already muted by the swish of tails
Combining with the trace-chains' lusty chink,
As snorting nostrils brought both sound and smell
Together in a welter of delight
In sensitivity, as turned the earth
To free the yearning mind from all despair.

Then later, resting on a grassy bank,
Rejoicing in the freedom from the streets,
He failed to notice how the pigeon's coo
Had lulled the warning cry of carrion crow.
All bust and bum in her brown overalls,
The buxom Brenda bustled on him there.
How tired you are and too concerned, she said:
Come drink this tea and eat this buttered bread.

She gave attention that she might receive;

A farmer's daughter and an only child,
She was concerned to make her farming pay,
She speculated with a view to gain
As much as possible without much loss
In either wealth or personality;
She schemed to gain the upper hand in all
She could without harm to herself, although
She never minded suffering some pain
As long as, in the end, she came out top,
In all ways making sure not to offend.
Consideration was her second name.
As Shulver ploughed and sowed across the fields,
She carefully attended to his needs.

Lying in the barn among the hay,
Many times did they have it away.
Shulver loved the comfort Brenda brought;
She's the one for me, that's what he thought,
Till he heard one day, to his alarm,
Brenda had intent to get his farm.
Treating him as if he were a sprat,
Best digested by her firm dictat,
Good for nothing but to be her jerk,
Moulding him, she made use of his work.
Sensing soon that he was being used,
Shulver scarpered, leaving her confused.
Beset by sodden skies then Shulver rode
Across the folding, dark November hills
As, slanting over soaking, rain-drenched slopes,
His pony squelched its way through mossy turf,
Until the haunting sound of cold wind pipes,
Rose floating high above the heather beds.

Her sheep-skinned shoulders warm from weeping winds,
And Cossack-trousered, wearing pillbox hat,
Nerina, booted, on her pony sat
Above him on a knoll, her pipes in voice
As, on her back, her quivered arrows slept,
Whilst, close at hand, her longbow lay at rest.

As pony hooves disturbed a sitting hare,
Nerina aimed her bow and shot it dead;
And then dismounting, taking up her kill,
She recognised her Shulver and stood still.

As beside peach blossom tea is sipped,
So Nerina paused, waiting her chance;
So Nerina paused, waiting to dance,
Wondering if Shulver had forgot.

Shaky as a cuckoo's notes in June
Shulver voiced: How come you tend the sheep?
How come that such as you are trusted
On these hills for so severe a task?

Piercing as a leopardess,
Sparkling as a sun-drenched sea,
Doleful as a dumb dog's eyes,
Glowing as a planet's light,
Subtle as a lapwing's flight,
Flashing her teeth, Nerina made reply:
Who can hunt and kill and cook?
Who can dance in any nook?
Who can count sheep to the last?

Who can brave the winter blast?
Who can train a collie dog?
Who can build a house of log?
Why, Nerina, she's the girl;
Watch her leap and twist and twirl;
Watch her now and raise a shout;
Watch her till your eyes drop out!

Kicking high, Nerina leapt the knolls,
Palm to toe and toe to palm she danced.
Yelling, Shulver jumped onto the ground;
Dashing in, he swept her in his arms.

Round his waist her booted legs she gripped,
Out and backward threw her arms and head.
Bending knee, he skipped her in a twirl;
Throwing her, he caught her on the fall;
Lifting her, he caught her in the air.
See! I dance as well as you, my dear!

The beckoning twilight shape of shepherd's hut
Drew near as they danced on towards its warmth,
That welcomed them with collie's beating tail
To stable both their mounts and make a meal.
Then haunted night, shade-writhed and hunting-prone,
Descended, pressurising fear to act
Upon those unprepared, who dare to move
Around within the dark, leaf-rotting tomb
Of drear November's activating womb.

Sigh desired delight

Sigh blurred the borders of dawn
Stifling the senses in mists
Where no patience is.

Sigh coughed blood through flared nostrils
Scenting only the fear of delay
Unheeding the sickly scent of death.

Sigh passed through darkness
Over fresh-dug graves.

Sigh purred with feline breath over rough tongues,
Rasping tissue,
Grating through the last fibres
Before delayed burial.

Sigh tumbled, gasping for air,
Stylised by deodorants,
Drenched in sweat and piddled pants.

Sigh slipped in under a wave.
No one suspected.
After the crash, sigh became a hysterectomy.

Sigh sobbed at the unnecessary
Ensconced deep in a slit trench
Dug deeper than Everest.

Sigh sighed over crowds grasping at straws
Farted from the arses of over-blown bull frogs
Pontificating from hidebound hideaways.

Sigh gasped at the nigh-high thigh
Inviting an escapade
Uncovered by laughter.

Sigh drifted into sleep.
Deluged by dream sauce, it awoke,
Creaming the tonsils of an over-ripe oyster.

Sigh on a knife edge
Slithered sideways into the East Wind.
Whispering, it sheltered under a blade of grass.

Soothing the silence with perceptive wafting,
Sigh sat beside a knot of knapweed.

Sigh moved softly through the fragrant night,
Anticipating climax,
After mating, fulfilment.
Concealed in contentment at the dawn of enigma
Sigh expresses disaster in the face of desire,
Success in the face of disaster.

*

Enwombed forever over barley fields waving goodbye,
Shulver breathed the sea beyond the hills,
Beyond the seal-goddessed rocks.

Nerina streamed her thighs
Like oceaned seals, softly firm
And seeking sustenance in stressful seas.
Fleecing the waves, she surfaced;

Skiffing over the skipping sea
She was seal-woman, weaving with barley waves.

Life became a sea
Sealed in a skin of heathered barley
Bounded by a rock-walled womb.

Now

Whitened were the heathered hillsides,
Wintered by the drifting snow,
When two lovers, walking, whispered
Words pretending all is now

Burning were the toiling turf fires
Bathing faces in their glow;
Beautifying fleeting moments,
Blessing them beyond the now.

Slowly spread the melting springtime;
See the lad's soft sadness grow;
Searching long to find his lover,
See him seek the seeping now.

Thistles grew between the wheat stalks,
Thoughtless fingers wiped the brow;
Throbbing need dispelled the sorrows,
Throwing all into the now.

Ripened well the wheat for harvest;
Reaped the golden soldiers' show;
Rent the safety of the womb-wall
Riven by the urgent now.

*

Disconsolate though not despairing,
Shulver stooked the sheaves.
Observations gave him quietude,

Considerations stalled his purpose.
When lethargic will, unwilling drooped,
Method accomplished tasks unmentionable.

Like bursting brackets pushed by brittle bricks,
Brichtina crunched across the stubbled field.

Shulver, see this daughter that I've bourn,
Fathered by you; do not look forlorn;
'Tis not too late; we can still be wed;
Say the word and no more need be said.

On the farm, Brichtina, you would wilt;
You lie better 'neath a city quilt;
In your city I would never thrive,
Anymore than bees without a hive.

Since you left I've been nigh destitute;
If you won't support me, you're a brute;
Soon the justice shall be told the same;
That's the way to stop your little game.

Speak, Brichtina, tell him what you will;
Speak to him of me for good or ill;
Marry you I will not that's for sure;
Maintenance I'll willingly endure.

So Brichtina had to be content;
Shulver gave her keep and paid her rent.
Later on she wed a totter man,
Calling rag and bone behind his van.
Brenda's father Coy

Showed no surprise on learning
Of her pregnancy:
His leathery old chops crinkled
In a gaping grin.

Patiently he waited for the birth.
When his granddaughter was six weeks old
He visited old Shiner, Shulver's father.

Shiner, dear old friend,
This union will bring us more security
Through the merging of our lands.

Shiner shook his head.
What price security?
A momentary dam,
Stemming the fretful sea.
Two into one will cram
More mass into a press,
Swelling against the gate,
Increasing more the stress,
Hastening dark fate
Imposed by selfishness.

COY
Resting here in false security,
Philosophy rides easy on the lips.

SHINER
Security does not arise in my condition;
For I say a man rests only in the mind.

Since a man fears to lose his cushions,
Too much security breeds insecurity.

COY
How so when small farms fail to pay?
For our children's sake we should amalgamate.

SHINER
If a man owned the whole earth,
Finding it too small,
He'd want the moon.

COY
Surely, Shiner, for the baby's sake,
Our children should be wed?

SHINER
Better a good father at a distance
Than an indifferent husband.

COY
It seems then, Shiner that you do not wish this match:
Do you not accept my daughter has been wronged?

SHINER
What is wrong?
Is it wrong to love today?
To hate tomorrow?
Our children loved their today:
Why should they now be forced
To live in tomorrow?

Even with her child
Other farmers' sons would be happy
To consider Brenda.
She's noted for her industry;
Your farm for its fertility.

COY
Does Shulver then object
To marrying my daughter?

SHINER
I do not know;
Let him answer for himself.
But, come now Coy, and lunch with me,
And let us talk of other things.

Shulver saw a white owl
Soft over willows.

Owl wings brushed his face
In the blanketing dusk.

He became a feather
Lifted by the woof of a stone dropping
In a pit full of feathers.

Wafted up
He was snared by weathered door grooves.

Later, he lined a sparrow's nest
The fledgling bodies warmed him

He longed to teach them to fly.

Marriage fell before him, unconsidered.
It was a stone falling into a pit of feathers.

Brenda rocked the cradle
Over the fields of two farms.

An elder bush,
Scrawny with early aging,
Explored the foundations of the farmhouse.

Under its skeletal arms
A toad sat feasting
On the listless flies of late summer.

Leaning out from the lattice,
Brenda plucked the elder berries.
The chubbiness of the toad pleased her.

His back reminded her
Of expanding farmland.

Marriage was elderberry wine
Anointing a toad's back.
There would be no escape for the listless.

*

It's November once again.
Shulver rides dejectedly into the hills.
He goes to negotiate the purchase of a horse.

He hopes to reach the distant vale by nightfall.
He thinks of Nerina.
If he cannot find her again soon
He feels he must wed Brenda in the spring.
As he enters the valley, the wind rises.
Already it's growing dark.
Riding towards the lights appearing in the village,
He identifies with the wind.

On unsteady feet
The wind fringes the pit.

Hanging by its heels
It shrieks into the abyss.

Losing its hold
It blunders, like a drunken sculptor,
Round boulders and red rocks.

Beauty is enhanced by frustration

So shall my striving be made bold in the rock face.

Shulver is the wind.
His fingers raking the rocks.
Rock chunks spin outwards.
As he struggles with the rock,
He longs for it to have hair.

Reaching around him,
He sweeps the air for substance.
Wisps entwine his hands.
Another air is breathing;
Warm blackness envelopes him.

The wind is dropping.
Redness blossoms through the haze
As calm enfolds him.
Her hair grown long, Nerina
Bears her lips to his and sighs.

Your pony stumbled;
It's safe in the lean-to.
Near here, on the path,
I found you clasping a rock.
You were knocked out by the fall.

Why did you leave me?
Nerina, are you not mine?
We should be married.
Shulver no; we have no need;
I've born your boy; he binds us.

Nerina talked with Shulver long into the night:
She disagreed with him concerning marriage.

Marriage is a mere convenience,
Invented by paternal totem-tanks,
That people might be better ordered
Through administrators, party politics and priests,
Lawyers, gimmicked rectitude, advertisement and aids.
Where real affection rules it is superfluous,
Where it does not, no more than imposition,
Grinding out the vestiges of self-respect
In long mistaken attitudes described as duty.

What we are, we are;
The essence of us speaks aright to us;
But, all too often masked, it struggles to survive,

As still it does for you, for me and for our child.
So let us then be true to this: the Essence of Our Mind;
For, when all other bonding breaks, it holds secure.

EPILOGUE

Astonished that Red Boar had ceased to speak
Before Man, seemingly, had found his place,
This man stood still to question him the while,
Complaining that his tale had no real end;
But Boar was adamant; his tale was done;
Although he had some more to add ad lib
Concerning Womankind and Wombfulness.

See here, said he, this circle made of stones,
Each standing firm, its entrance over there?
This represents the Womb of Mother Earth,
And more than that, the Universal Womb.
This being so, no tale can have an end,
Nor yet, beginningless, begin at all,
Except in this, that where we take it up,
It seems as if it started on its way,
From where it first fell on our eager ears.

The Womb churns out, takes back, casts out again,
In ever whirling, changing forms,
Deceiving all in multitudes of flux.
This, in reality, is truthfulness
Relating one to all and everything that is,
That was and evermore will be until
The Now is realised like the Bones of Boar,
Which move-less, move throughout eternity,
Without a thought for either start or stop.

Since end, beginning, have no meaning here,
Come, Wombfulness, deliver us from fear.

HERE ENDS THE SAGA OF THE RED BOAR

JENNY

Was there another end beyond
The sights that once she saw?
Or was her endless end no more
Than her beginning when
She rode the ice floes of indifference?
Certain of her capabilities,
She felt no fear as then she braved
The salty torrent's tempting, tortuous course
To jump judiciously
From icy plate to plated lumps of ice.
Fearful, they called her back;
But she rode on beguiled
By life's long, wandering wiles.

Sprightly she sprang the spuming
Waves wild wandering lust,
As lingering, she lay about their threatening thrust
With arm, leg, oar and sail,
Relating to the elements with fearless pride.

And so she dealt with life
In every crevice of its vagaries.
As fearless on the foam she forged her form,
So bravely does she beam her brightness
Into all-embracing, universal unity.

PREFERENCES

I would prefer to live in a brick house
built with my own hands
and having a tall chimney
rising above the woodlands.
I would clothe the winter nights
in long white candles and flames
fingering up from the broad hearth
stacked with fragrant logs and old frames,
dry and brittle to get the fire going;
and I would boil a kettle full of water for tea
to sip as I conjured up from the blaze, lilting songs
and magical tales of the earth, the sky and the rolling green sea.
I would keep no one who would be offended
at muddy boots and the floor would be such
as not to be bothered by trivia
or to have need of sweeping too much;
and I would feel free, if it suited my purpose,
to spit through the flames without soiling my beard,
and it wouldn't concern me at all
if there were those who considered me weird;
for I would make potions of herbs and keep bees
and many folk would visit my room
seeking advice on all manner of things
bothering them this side of the tomb.

It would be my desire that some would sit
in the flickering light of the fire
and listen in awe to my tales

and songs accompanied by harp and by lyre.
Sparkling black rooks would build
in their hundreds around my red house
and I wouldn't mind too much
the lost and occasional mouse.

A wolf would lie at my door
and be my companion in need
as in the grey forest we wandered
untrammelled by dogma or creed.
I would make my own shoes from the hide of a deer
and shoot with a bow
made of yew and know how to grow things
and mend clothes and learn how to sew;
and on long summer days I'd sit with my wolf
by my side on the top of a knoll
and see the blue of the sky as the mind case of life
and the clouds as the merging grey thoughts of its soul.

The Artist

In the drop of the deep night
Towards the bedrock of beauty
Shades engrave the multitudes with light

The horse rolls back the plains with thunder
Sweating light from his flanks
Over the galloping grasses
Whose echoing multitudes
Darken the earth with survival.

The fire was coloured before it burst
The horse from a cleft in the bedrock
Boiling the grasses in the juice of his rumbling guts

The sun sings under the shadow of the painter's brush

Dolly

Dolly dash your bottom
In the hearth glow's warming light,
Dance around the table
Through the twilight into night.

Dance now with the Goddess
As she teaches us to share,
Turning us to star dust
In her womb of constant care.

Bringing forth her children,
With a sigh of deep content,
See how she devours them
When their span of life is spent.

Dash again, dear Dolly,
Woman, maiden, priestess, wife,
Clad in constant beauty
Through the orchard of this life.

Gather now the apples
From the branches overhead;
Scatter them in circles
Till both life and death are fed.

Wolf Man

Overcoming cares and complications
Three men come to me for their separate
Assignments, but only one is wolf-like,
Wary and decidedly diffident,
Unsure of himself – the others rampant,
Ready, willing and wanting to do it,
Whereas he fawns faithfully, loyalty
His watchword, lap leaning, licking his way,
Seeking reality in reassurance,
Wanting to please me, panting for pleasure;
But mine, not his. Selflessly savouring
The scene of my enticing attitudes,
His satisfaction eagerly erupts,
Exploded by my joyful ecstasy.

THE POT

The pot was not al-
Together symmetrical:
Finger instilled grooves
Circled its inclinations
Beyond its ability

When pouring, water
Did not run down outside it,
Though it had no spout;
Through the joy in its making,
There was beauty in its use.

It was natural,
Acquainted with the wrist pulse
Of its creator,
Who made it in harmony
With a rhythmic universe.

The Three Visitors

Tread softly, softly,
Softly tread along the garden path
And then before me bow,
Bow low your noble head,
Your head so noble in its rustic charm;
For I have spoken with the wild east wind;
And I am king once more,
And rule again across the rolling fields
Here islanded by clumps of leafing trees.

Be careful, careful,
Careful where you place your naked feet,
And set your pitcher down,
Down here among the flowers,
The ice-white flowers of man's indifference;
For I have ridden on the east wind's back
And fear the ice no more,
But melt it in the arms of my embrace
To torrent it across the sweeping plains.

Move gently, gently,
Gently move amongst the gloating gulls,
And touch their outstretched wings,
Outstretched to greet the sky,
The battle dome of life's disharmony;
For I have seized the east wind's shouting song,
The Vikings' battle cry,
And wed it to the weird loon's mating call
To form the music of the turning spheres.

Too Old

'Too old,' they said, 'The lights are not for you.'
'Moonlight is mine,' she said, 'To ride or rue.
'See here the silver stair's entrusting thrust
'That beckons me to linger, love and lust.'

'My colour fades and suitors may seem few
'Among the dainty daisies drenched in dew
'Laid low amidst the mown meanderings
'Of many mutilated fairy rings;
'But hearken! Hear the hooting owl call home
'My last lone lover who has long since come
'To rest within my bower's heaving breast,
'And will not leave until he's stood the test
'Of stamina enshrined between my thighs,
'Empowered beyond a thousand heaving sighs.'

APOLOGIES

                        I do apologise;
I realise now I should have been more gentle
About the way I walked upon the grass;
To rob the thrush was never my intention;
How could I notice when I slimed the worm,
Or when I crushed the slowly moving snail?
It seemed I walked so softly in the twilight,
So well intentioned was my every step;
I never realised one could harm so many
By doing nearly nothing in the dark.

Movement

Was she with it, he wondered
Or was he withered without her?
And would she be bothered
Better than before he knew her?

When questioned she quibbled:
When asked about her achievements,
She thoroughly threw him
With a blather of bereavements.

Consider me concerned, he said.
In silence she softened
Resolute, he ran to her rear
Resolving not to be ruffled.

Throwing her thoughts at him through her
Thonged buttocks, she quivered.
He quibbled, but she was certain,
Disdainful as she delivered.

Wait! Whither away wench? He called.
Love's lost on you, she said.
You receive without realising
What meanderings mean.
Fostering forms, you falsify
Reality, ruling out
Discernment, dreams and destiny
For the dust of delight.

What moves when the flag flies:
Fresh fabric, whiplash wind or mind?
What moves when the wench walks:
Body, legs, mincing mindfulness,
Or something deeper still?
Who knows? We are but the victims
Of each circumstance and follow
That which bids us: come away!

FIRE HORSE

Once amongst the grass there burst this flame
Glancing sharply upwards at the clouds,
It longed to lick out patterns like they did.

Soon it wove around the growing grass,
But did not burn it up as one might think.

Instead it copied how the grasses grew
And blended green with red
To form a whispering hayscape
Like unheeding hair
Before the flickers of a rising breeze
That later blew into a whining storm.

The earth heaved up
And grass and fire together came to be
The mane and tale of one tremendous horse,
Who tossed his head into the clouds
And split himself like them
To rain fire horses everywhere upon the plain.

Imbolc

Though the buds remain unopened,
Cosy, patient for escape,
Couched inside in gendered greeting
Life is lilting into shape.

Gathered now within the silence,
Quicken quietly for the quest:
Sons and daughters gather wisdom,
Striving always for the best.

Goddess please bring forth the fresh life
From the womb of winter cold,
Let the newborn find a welcome
In the warmth of nature's fold.

Not too late and not too little,
Not too soon and not too fast;
May the new life brightly burgeon,
Feeding future from the past.

May the hag meet with the newborn,
Merging then and now as one;
Teaching us to know and cherish
End is what has just begun.

The Three Wives

Pub ensconced and cornered by the bar,
Three men furtively discussed their wives.

The first to speak was large,
Rounded like a barrel,
His eyebrows bristling like bunches of birch twigs,
His head bald as a trounced track
Blasted through a bed of rushes.

The second was dreamy and diffident,
Grey jowled and preoccupied
With matters of seeming great concern,
Which smothered his shoulders,
Rounding them like a whipped willow wand.

The third was a bright, cheery fellow
With a twinkle in his eye:
A fugitive from a fork-lift truck.

FIRST MAN

My wife is a pneumatic drill
Ripping through the bones of my brain case:
The noise stops only to recommence with renewed vigour:
The road into my mind lies like a scattered mass of rubble:
She never stops to repair it,
Nor does she ever think of building a new one.

SECOND MAN

My wife is like a block of high rise flats
Never sure of her own level:
Attempting to look out of three windows at once,
She falls flat on her face before the fungus worshipping planners
And complains when I fail to find time to co-operate
In her search for neighbourliness.

THIRD MAN

My wife is a fork lift truck
Unloading a consignment of life seed:
She pushes in with a swing,
Heaves and lifts high,
Backs out, drops and re-positions
Until the last drop of the commodity is lodged
In the warehouse of her contentment.

WIND HORSE

See how the wind paints it portrait
Over all the earth.
The horse sees the wind:
It is the ubiquitous toss of mane and tail
Through the boiling air,
Like dying grass flaming round a tree,
Or fingerprints endlessly patterned
Over a racing skyscape.

The west wind is the thunder of hooves;
The north wind is a whinnying icicle;
The south wind is a mare in season;
Only the east wind is visible.
It is mirrored in the horse's eye;
It is the seat of his power.
He is wind horse,
The shifting seat of landscape,
And the eye in the earth's face.

The Provider

Curved and calling me she stood entwined
With honeysuckle creeping close around
Her heaving breasts and eager, silken thighs.
The tune of her desire was played by her;
I had no part in it. Do what I might,
The steps I danced were hers, not mine, to move
Around the circle of her aptitude.
She learned from me and leaned upon my loins
To drain me dry in destiny's dark ditch
Now dank with pert, decrepit platitudes.
Mellow was her mindfulness and more
Than I could mind. I was the path to be
Explored by her; she was no path for me
To wend my way to her eternity.
She wanted mine and took it fast and firm
To juice her future with her own desire
To have it all her way and I to wait
Upon her every need. Did she need me?
Maybe in her own way but not in mine.
Provider was my niche and hers was me.

Cow Pleasure

Here is the delicious sound
of a cow cropping fresh grass:
she flicks her tongue round a wodge,
presses up with her teeth, tugs,
and pulls with a satisfied
sucking crunch and swallows fast
into her cavernous depths.

Her firm tread is red-heavy
under her dewlap's quiver,
ponderous and ox-sure like
her ancestors who plodded,
pulling the plough over this
same pasture she now grazes
observing with cloud eyes.

Her mooing is mellow deep
like old gongs from Tibetan
temples and tranquil yaks
undeterred by adverse winds.
her life is tongue grasped lushness
fortifying maternal
feeling in long lactations

ended only by a bolt's
fast thud. Her pleasure will not
end in pain, decrepitude
and tasteless sheets; but then, she
cannot ever know the joy
it is to stand here watching
her enjoy the juice-filled grass.

Bodiless Head Speaks

This stone head was carved
So long since that no one knows
Whether it was hand,
Wind, water, frost or sand
That tied its curly hair in bows.

Its face is rotund,
Greenish, like a full-cheese moon,
Matured to sustain
Beyond the thinking brain,
The heart of wisdom in a rune.

Its deep-slashed grimace
Utters fertile words to all,
Rich and liquid warm,
Fresh-fed from goddess form,
For those who heed its silent call.

Its wandering curls
Devise art's deviousness:
Its pondering eyes,
Perceiving latent sighs
Disperse all pain with their caress.

High on the wall side,
Lustily this head looks down,
Ageless in its charm,
Its gaze so warm
More so than any saint in golden gown.

The Girl in the Kiosk

The girl in the kiosk
serves, tea, coffee, buns, sausage rolls
and all kinds of ices with deft, supple fingers
and flashing blue eyes;
but no one can guess that she does
clever things with her hands
when she's home in her flat by the sea.

The girl in the bed-sit
carves cosy-nosed bears for her bedside
to growl her to sleep and nuzzle her warm
through the cold winter nights
and cuddle her close from her frosty
white fears that strive
to extinguish the smile of her trust.

The girl in the window
carves feather-finned fish in her
grandmother's ingle-nooked, fire-flooded,
hearth-centred home, angled close
in the meeting of old roads with new,
where the hunting brown owl hoots over the burn
of the traffic's fast flow.

No, there's none who can guess
that the girl in the kiosk is not just a girl,
but an artist who sees in a ham roll
the shape of a hungry wild beast
she has to create in the night
with her knife that chips bits
from the wood she picks up in the park.

Natural Balance

The leaping hillside
Grasps the striving hare,
Hurtling it haze-ward
Beyond the snowline.

The scarred earth fondles
The fervent wolf pack
Speeding it beast-ward
Beneath the cloud roof.

The wolf drags no wheel,
Nor the hare a plough;
Noses nudge where fate
Shatters destruction.

Let Go

Go forth into the night to find the day;
Depart, return; there is no other way;
Accept what is as part of what shall be
And was. The endless end evaporates, is free
From nothingness, from form, from clinging on
To aimless thoughts, to all that's come and gone.

Wolf

Wolf is the wheat grain
Growing on a moving belt,
Passing the forests
Hungry for earth sustenance,
Nevertheless selective.

Wolf is a deep well,
Full of fact and fathomless;
Dark and defiant
Chained to the fluid purpose
Of revitalisation.

Wolf is a fresh flower,
The point of a pyramid
And unpluckable:
His howl is the perfumed night;
His petals are star-coloured.

Thinking he knows wolf,
Man shoots him with an arrow
And becomes afraid
When the dead eyes stare at him.
Gibbering, he slinks away.

Man turns into a wolf;
He bites; misses; wounds himself;
Then, howling with pain,
He runs round screaming MURDER!
And turns back into a man.

Bleeding profusely,
He stumbles into the forest,
Not understanding
When Wolf feeds him on warm milk
And licks his wounds, healing him.

Wolf is a clear pool
Fed through the spring of his eyes
From the far-flung stars.
He smiles as he wags his tail,
Brushing the leaves from the trees.

Gathering the leaves
He digs a cavernous den,
Lining it with them.
His pink mouth is a deep cave,
Leaf-lined with growling laughter.

Wolf regurgitates,
Feeding his den-cosy cubs.
Slowly teaching them:
Man retches and rends his throat;
His children are less well taught.

Wolf is the dark night
With a million piercing eyes;
He sees everything:
Winter trembles before him
As he speeds over the plains.

Lord of the tundra,
The caribou worship him;
His surgeon-white teeth
Restore health to their herdlings,
Protecting their heritage.

Wolf is the god-beast,
The doom-killing All-Father,
Worshipped by all beasts;
Lucid across the clear air,
His mind rules the wilderness.

RESIDUES

Residue is grubby faced, a child in tears,
Bewildered
At the grown up laughter over drinks.

Residue is this old man who lives alone;
Laughter is his scalded cat,
Who screeches when he, inadvertently,
Spills tea about its ears.

Happiness is when the child finds solace
In the old man's dreams and shares his tea.

No one here complains when tea leaves splash the door,
Or when they pet the cat
And let it drink from china cups upon the floor.

All else is residue to these two friends,
As now they sit and share
The laughter, tears and tea leaves round the door.

The Gasp

Once
there was
this gasp

It was
the wisp of fire
that lit the lantern
that revealed the secrets
of forbidden cities
unbelieved delights.

It was
the breath of air
that blew the jasmine
that enriched the purpose
of this present beauty's
unconcealed desire.

It was
the moistened earth
that slimed the plumule
that explored the pathway
of increasing mind-light's
unrehearsed release.

It was
the gasp that spread
the finite to infinity
before it banged its head
against creation's wall.

The Other Day

The other day when I awoke
The sparrows were my morning cloak.

The other day when I got up,
The orchard was my loving cup.

The other day when I went out,
The cuckoo was my morning shout.

The other day when I came home,
I found a girl within my room.

The other night when I lay down,
This girl, she was my dressing gown.

Susan

Wary, she wanders in her wonderland,
Wistfully wishing to relate to reality
In her own way – not theirs,
Ripe with rules and reckless in its rectitude.

Easing eagerly earthward,
Endlessly endeavouring to integrate,
Intense with earth scent
And easing into eeriness,
She encircles the erstwhile night
In the dawn of her desires.

Had she failed to face up to fact?
Or had she fled false fate
To find fascination in the fluctuations
Found only in the eager earthiness
Of everyday encounters
With the actualities of existence?

Happy in the heartland of her harvesting years,
She sings sense into solitude
And comfort into companionship,
Mingling the many with the meagre,
And merging the meagre with a multitude
Of cascading colours curtaining
The vagaries of the vanishing years
Passing before her into eternity.

Inferno

This lane is an inferno blazing flames
In every shade of green and grey around
Its tunnel walls where dancing light plays games
Through twigs and foliage and fire is found
Without the aid of orange, red or gold,
And burns far fiercer in its leaping arcs,
That twine the springing new into the old,
Than ever could a bonfire throwing sparks.
For here's a furnace where the faithful meet
With life's uncertain days. Is there a doubt
That conflict is the necessary heat
That bursts the bud and chips the fledgling out?
    As sure as sun designs the way of life,
        This lane snakes out its scorching path of strife.

Black Magic

When first I noticed him
he was a paper origami bird,
black and sitting in an old dead elm,
pictured stark within my window frame.
His body was composed of many wedges,
culminating in a hatchet beak,
which, when he opened it,
disintegrated him into a raucous rook,
who deftly snapped a twig and carried it away.

Later in the day I saw him with his tribe,
lay keels of many coracles
directly into branching waves
where, when commissioned, they will sail them
through the storms unharmed,
becoming high black leaping sails
or crewmen hatching other origami birds
to silhouette delight in window frames.

Hairdresser Horse

Horse is a hairdresser and
does not barber the grass. He
moulds it with his lips and tongue,
designing styles and shaping
shades that blend desire with dust
like dancing hair that plays at
hide and seek with laughing eyes.

The hairdresser is horse-like:
he grazes selectively
and gallops over the earth
with his tongue, stopping only
at fences erected by
his customers, who must be
carefully cultivated.

Scissor quick, earth-kicking hooves
ripple gloss from the flanks of
hairdresser horse as he moves,
tossing hair through deft fingers,
speech-feathered and supple, like
harness, close-moulding styles in
each hair that grows on our heads.

*

THE SACK

He hung there, a sack,
A sack full of potatoes,
Finger abrasive,
Bulging taut and nail catching,
Ripped open by a knife thrust.

One by one they dropped,
Juicy potatoes falling down,
Smacking the hard ground.
He hung there, an empty sack,
His resources drained away.

They left him hanging
And picked up the potatoes,
Gently, one by one.
They planted them everywhere;
They grew all over the world.

The sack just hung there,
A musty, rotting stench bag
Flapping in the wind.
They said it was alive,
But only the potatoes grew.

They rose rapidly,
A green mass of vomit weed,
Poisoning all truth:
In fact, lethal entities
Sprouting out of a proud mind.

They gathered them up,
These poison, grey potatoes,
And put them in sacks,
Which began to split open,
Making everyone angry.

Men fought over this crop:
Blighted earth apples,
Killing each other:
Ranting and ridiculing
In the name of love, they died.

The sack hung there still.
No one tried to cut it down:
They liked it that way;
They said it was still living,
And taught them how to love more.

Love was in the sack,
But most people preferred
The poison potatoes.
They left the sack hanging there.
God was very unhappy.

But he didn't do anything:
He wasn't made that way.

Neglect

Wistfully you wait within the garden;
Forlorn, you stand beneath the hawthorn trees,
Waiting there beside the ragged hedgerow,
Your hair attended by the gentle breeze.

Resting in neglect, the garden greets you;
Alone and unattended, it has peace:
Waving bluebells bloom beneath the birch trees
As if to say: *Neglect is not decease*.

Cease to strive and rest alone with beauty;
Let bluebells dance beside your golden hair
Deep inside, your sorrow is abiding:
Neglect it here and banish all your care.

SUFFOLK SHORES

I sailed my ship on Suffolk shores,
I sailed her through the trees,
I sailed her through the tall elm tops
Beside the velvet leas.

Her sails were made of drifting mist,
Her hull was made from soil,
Her masts were made of bronze sunlight,
Her cargo fruits of toil.

Her rudder was the black rook's wing,
Her captain, peasant pride,
Her crew were songs beside the sea
Sung by the surging tide.

Sense of Values

Do-good Morality made such a scene
Because Jemima danced in nothing but
A maypole ribbon made of crepe-de-chine.

He never said a word when Joshua
Evaded paying income tax and VAT,
Or when Alfredo couldn't get a flat.

One day I met this self-styled moralist
Attended by his faithful sycophants:
A dog in knickers and a pig in pants.

It all went well until, one day, the pig
Surprised his master with his trousers down
Cuddling Jemima in her dressing gown.

The Legend of the Unmade Primrose

Man made God
And ordered him to create the world.
God moved over the landscape
Leading his host,
Explaining everything
And telling the animals and plants he had created them.

The animals were annoyed
And tried to avoid God:
The plants were unperturbed:
But they all agreed with God
About the creation
Because they feared Man,
Who had the power to destroy them all
And himself.

But no one had noticed
A small yellow flower
Growing beside a stream.
She told God she had never been created
And was there only because of relationships.

God was furious and cursed the flower.
Man, not wanting to undermine the authority of his created god,
Seized the flower
And threw her into the woods.

Man uprooted the woods
And sowed corn to amass wealth;
But the yellow flower persisted under bushes.

Soon, her relations spread
All over the earth, growing everywhere,

Some yellowing the ditch banks in spring,
Where Man feverishly plucked them
As if seeking to eradicate a rash
In a long dream.

One day, a small boy came across the yellow flower
Under a hazel bush.
Stretching his fingers across the five-stalked blooms,
He named her Fivefingers.

Man was mad when the boy told him,
And so he created the Devil to plague God
And cause a Fall.

Unimpressed by these antics,
Fivefingers lifted her head and smiled.
Understanding her, the boy was enlightened.

*

The Singing Bowl

Hard as his work was, Hugh cherished his woodman's life. Accepting it as his earth-given lot, he found it free, wholesome and devoid of rancour. The yearly round of felling, lopping, planting, tending and coppicing was for him as the fiddle is to the bow. The time had been when he had lacked a wife to complete his bliss. Then, one day, Verdina had come to him lithe and laughing in her bouncing beauty. Wed by the waterfall, their joy had bubbled over; but now, in January, Hugh was filled with sorrow as he wandered alone in the white and leafless woods.

Verdina had fallen ill of a fever that had racked her for weeks. He had nursed her tenderly, preparing for her infusions of herbs, until she was well again. Sadly however, there was something that his herbal lore was unable to cure. The fever had left her face so wrinkled and parched, he could no longer bear to look at her. Too often he made excuses to go into the forest even when he would have been better occupied chopping wood for the fire instead of leaving it all for Verdana to do.

One day Hugh wandered into a part of the forest unfamiliar to him, which surprised him as he had supposed he knew it all so well. Presently, he found himself on the edge of a bowl-shaped hollow, treeless save for a score or so of gnarled hawthorn trees growing near a russet-walled cottage. A wraith of smoke, scarcely darker than the snow covering its gabled roof, wisped skyward from its crooked red chimney stack. The front door was ajar and the sound of creaky chanting issued forth from somewhere inside.

The haunting quality of the chant diverted Hugh's

attention away from the smoke, which was drifting towards the edge of the hollow. Creeping up on him, it wove around him, binding his arms to his sides. Like fine, white hair, it moved over him so rapidly he had no time to cry out before it covered his mouth. It was then the chanting ceased and a voice called to him: 'Why tarry on the edge? Come in, young man, come in!'

Gathering his wits together, Hugh attempted to run back into the forest, but to no avail. Such was the hair's strength it jerked him backwards off his feet and down into the hollow, shooting him like a greased sled over its shiny surface to bring him right up to the cottage door, which sprang wide open as he struck against it. A cackling laugh greeted him as he struggled to his feet inside the cottage. There in the inglenook sat an old crone, her eyes glowing fire and her white hair weaving around her and up the chimney like smoke. Lifting her black-clad arms, she began pulling her hair back down the chimney, causing Hugh to spin round like a top as it unwound from his body. Even when completely free of it, he continued to twirl. Ensnared in this wild dance, he was unable to break free from its rhythm. Reluctantly delighting in it, he tried to dance out through the doorway, but an icy blast slammed the door in his face.

Uttering a glass-shattering laugh, the crone began beating out another rhythm causing the dance to grow wilder. Then, just as Hugh thought it would dance him to death, a fresh sound akin to a doleful whine deluged his ears. As other doleful sounds competed with it there came a clit-clit-clatting noise that caused Hugh to clap his hands to his ears for the fear of it. Collapsing onto the floor, he cried out for the cacophony to cease. There followed a silence so deep in its stillness that it was even more frightening than the plethora of sound that had preceded it. Dragging himself to his knees, Hugh was on the point of screaming for the noise to cease when his gaze met that of the crone whose calm demeanour had the effect of embedding him within a kaleidoscope of coloured dream clouds.

When Hugh awoke it was to find that he had been sleeping on the hearth in a bed of the old woman's hair. The flame of her eyes illuminated the room better than any lamp and, as he gazed upon her, he became aware of the presence of an ageless beauty. In the lap of her dark robe the crone, now turned matriarch, held an alloyed metal bowl that reflected the light from her eyes to dance it around the room. Floor, walls, ceiling: all were covered with her hair.

As Hugh gazed in awe upon all this, a chortling sound issued forth from a cot in a corner of the room. Then, as he was about to investigate to find out if there was a baby there, his attention was drawn back to the matriarch who seemed to have grown taller. Moments later, the darkness fell from her to reveal a robe richly patterned in meandering reds, greens and gold after the fashion of life in an oak-wood. Rising from his bed, Hugh bowed in awe before such a goddess. This time when she spoke, her voice was ageless. 'Presently you will sleep again. When you awake you will find this bowl in your hands and with it a short, thick stick with knobbed ends. Return home and play the bowl before Verdina your wife, who will dance for you and your joy will be restored. But remember never to strike the bowl in anger. However, you may tap, stroke and beat it, coaxing from it the music of life and it will immerse you in the power of the silence rewarding you with universal wisdom, but strike it once in anger and I will return to reclaim it.'

Hugh sank back into a deep and dreamless sleep. When he again awoke, Crone, cottage, hawthorns and hollow had all disappeared and he was seated under a vast oak tree, his hands clasped round both bowl and stick. Supposing he had spent the night in the forest, he hastened home expecting to find Verdina distraught with anxiety at his long absence. 'How soon you've returned!' she said. 'I hadn't thought to see you again till dusk.' Then, setting eyes on the gleaming bowl, she was overjoyed. Hugh told her he had found it near an oak tree.

After supper, Hugh took up the bowl giving it a few tentative taps with its stick. The ringing tones trembled Verdina's body into a desire to dance. Gaining confidence, Hugh stroked the stick around inside the bowl creating a plethora of delectable sounds. Then, as Verdana danced before him, he thought he had never before seen such beauty. So it was that night their love bond was fully restored.

On awaking the following morning, Hugh was distressed to find Verdina's skin as wrinkled as ever; but she didn't seem to mind. 'Today is the first of February; we mustn't look back,' she said.

After that, as the days passed, Verdina's appearance no longer troubled Hugh as he became ever more skilled at playing the bowl and her dancing increased in both joy and beauty. With the advent of May everything everywhere began to sparkle as if the whole world were echoing the joy of the singing bowl and Verdana conceived. The following February she gave birth to a golden haired daughter she named Maia, who was clapping and skipping in time to the bowl's singing before she was two years old.

As Maia grew she prospered with her parents under

the guidance of the singing bowl. When she reached her fourth birthday, Hugh fetched children from the village in the valley to play with her. All went well until a child asked why Verdana wasn't smooth skinned like other mothers. So it was that evening when Hugh reached for the bowl to play it, Maia asked him about her mother's skin. Rushing outside into the starlight, Hugh angrily struck the bowl as he cried out: 'Are we never to be free from this curse!' The bowl flashed lightning, thunder crashed and a mighty wind blasted Hugh high into the air and head over heels. The earth disappeared. He stopped breathing. He was gazing into a vast, star-studded bowl. Was it above him? Was it below him? It was impossible to tell. For everywhere he looked it was into the bowl. He closed his eyes. When he opened them again it was to find himself plummeting towards the outside of a much smaller, inverted bowl. It was the earth. Plump! He had landed in a snowdrift not far from the cottage. Picking himself up, he ran back home. Running to greet him, Verdana cried: 'Did you see her? Did you see her?'

Hugh didn't understand. 'See whom?'

'The tall, long haired woman clad in a red, gold and green robe. She seized Maia and sped into the night.'

Overwhelmed with sorrow, Hugh guided Verdina back into the cottage where, as the lamplight illuminated her face, he saw that the wrinkles had all disappeared leaving her face as beautiful as the when he had first set eyes on her.

Hugh and Verdina never saw the singing bowl again, but three more children were born to them, each one of them in the month of February. It was as if hope were returning to them as the days lengthened. The years passed and, on a Midsummer's Day when the children were all well grown they went with them singing and dancing through a hawthorn grove and out into a woodland glade where, at the height of their merry making, they fancied they were joined by a red-lipped and green-clad damsel with golden hair.

That night as Hugh and Verdina stood gazing upwards into the vastness of the star-studded bowl, its silence spoke to them. Peace possessed them. Truth had become one with joy and fulfilment was theirs.

THE END of THE SINGING BOWL

*

TAMSIN AND THE WOLF

Tamsin's best friend was a grey wolf. Whenever he appeared on late spring days the bumble bees seemed to buzz more merrily. So she called him Beasey. Early each morning he was waiting outside when she opened the door of her cabin on the edge of a great forest and she would throw her arms round him and hug him as he licked the sleep from her eyes with his warm tongue.

Without Beasey's help Tamsin would have found it difficult to survive. She had no brothers or sisters and her parents had died of a mysterious disease over a year ago. Beasey had first appeared a week after their funeral. Initially frightened, Tamsin then noticed a dead rabbit lying on the doorstep. When she picked it up, Beasey wagged his tail and trotted back into the forest.

Tamsin cooked the rabbit and ate it. From then on Beasey brought her gifts of food three or four times a week. Encouraged by his support she worked away in the garden, grew vegetables and foraged in the forest for herbs, roots, berries and nuts. Whenever she strayed too far Beasey would appear and guide her safely back home.

One morning Beasey wasn't there when Tamsin opened the cabin door. Concerned, she decided to look for him. Carefully combing her long golden hair, she braided it into a pigtail. Donning her green cloak and skull cap, she set out walking fast in her bright red boots. The forest was unusually quiet and she wondered why no birds were singing on such a bright morning. Presently, unnerved by the persistent silence, she glanced behind her. Stopping in her tracks, she turned round and gasped. Wherever she had walked she had left bright red footprints. Sitting on a large log, she removed one of the boots. It looked the same as it always did. Beasey had brought her the boots a few weeks ago. Replacing the boot, she shrugged and continued on into the forest. Presently she found herself walking in an avenue of hawthorns that soon closed in overhead until it was like being in a long, dimly lit tunnel.

Strangely elated, Tamsin felt compelled to go on. After a while it grew lighter and she found herself in a large glade surrounded by mighty oaks. A chilling breeze plucked at her green cloak. In vain she sought to wrap it close around her. The breeze strengthened into a wind. Snatching the cap from her head, it billowed the cloak into a great green circle. Seizing her pigtail, it unravelled it, causing her hair to dance around her like a ripened cornfield. Then, lifting her out of her boots, it whirled her round, faster and faster.

Tamsin was soon dancing off the ground and up into the tops of the oaks where her robe became a leaf-like canopy pierced by the light of her hair. Then her body became a branch and her eyes became a myriad of oak catkins that gazed out from the midst of her hair into the glade's inviting fertility. The pain of being stretched out made her cry and her tears watered the grass.

'O that Beasey's tongue might lick the pain from my eyes!' she cried. But her bare feet held her firmly to the trunk. Her efforts to walk down the trunk and onto the ground where her red boots lay were to no avail. The wind slackened back into a breeze and, suddenly, the glade was filled with mocking laughter. Then a voice called: 'Without your boots you must stay there, stay there, there until the woodland drum is beaten with a green stick, until you learn to come and go as the flowing of milk and until you can smell the scent of starlight.'

'Alas!' sighed Tamsin. 'Then I must stay here forever.

Although I may be able to find a drum, how can my body learn to flow like milk and how shall I ever smell the perfume of the stars?'

'Look!' mocked the voice. 'Look at the forest floor.'

As Tamsin looked her heart was broken. There on the flattened grass lay a wolf-skin. She knew then why Beasey hadn't come to her that morning. The voice spoke no more and she was left to endure her grief in helpless silence.

Later that day a peasant lad entered the glade. Seeing the wolf-skin, he picked it up and threw it over his shoulder. Then, gathering up the red boots, he followed the red footprints back into the hawthorn tunnel. Continuing to follow them, he reached Tamsin's log cabin, where he lost all knowledge of his former life. So he stayed there, tending the garden, cleaning the cabin and planting trees in the forest.

Spring grew into summer and summer ripened into autumn. During all that time the peasant saw no one. His only companion was an old raven who accompanied him into the forest showing him where to find firewood and the best places to catch rabbits. Towards the end of October the peasant wrapped the wolf-skin around him to keep out the cold. On the last night of the month, with the sky bright with stars, the old raven came and pecked at the cabin door.

'Bring the red boots and follow me into the forest,' he said.

Wrapping himself in the wolf-skin, the peasant obeyed. The raven led him along the hawthorn tunnel and back into the oak tree glade where the green cloak had blown away and Tamsin was shivering with cold. Looking inside a hollow tree at the raven's bidding, the peasant found a drum and a green stick. Seating himself in the centre of the glade, he began to beat out a rhythm. The breeze strengthened, mocking him with savage laughter; but the raven started croaking and the peasant increased the tempo. There followed much grunting and squealing as a large black sow entered the glade and lay on her side to suckle her piglets. As the milk began to flow, the glade was filled with music and merry laughter as men and maidens danced their way into it. Ceasing its mockery, the breeze howled itself up into a blustering wind. The peasant beat harder, the raven croaked louder, the sow increased the flow of her milk and the revellers danced faster until the wind gave up.

As Tamsin watched the sow and piglets she felt herself flowing in and out as if she were both giving and receiving milk. 'I'm flowing like the milk,' she said. 'And the drum is being beaten with a green stick. If only I could smell the starlight I would be free.'

There followed a wild cry. A naked figure leapt out from among the dancers and stabbed the peasant in the heart with a long knife. The green stick cracked and, howling like a wolf, the peasant leapt up, throwing the red boots high in the air. Alarmed, Tamsin took a deep breath. Then, as the night filled her lungs, she could smell the starlight. Running down the oaken trunk, she caught the red boots as they fell and put them on. All the revellers had disappeared. And there was Beasey, sitting in the centre of the glade and howling up at the stars. Running to him, Tamsin threw her arms round his neck. Ceasing his howling, he licked the summer sleep from her eyes. On the forest floor Tamsin noticed a russet coloured cloak and skull cap. She put them on.

'Follow me!' croaked the raven. He led them back to the cabin and the sow and piglets followed. And, as far as I know, sow, raven, Tamsin and Beasey are all living happily there to this very day.

THE END of TAMSIN and the WOLF

THE POLYTHENE TUNNEL

Ribs protrude through taut stretched skin
Transparent in the sunlight,
Revealing beneath, pulsating life
Growing from rich flesh
Attached to a rock backbone.

Life giving life breeding life unlimited,
Sleeved and breathing beneath a ribbed roof,
An emaciated chest concealing wealth,
Breathing life within a sun-pierced skin.

Purposefully the girl polythenes the iron ribs,
Stretching tight the plastic sheet,
Protecting the plants;
Like a ferret she forages in the tunnel.

Caged in her own ribs,
She scrapes at the living flesh
Kneeling on her own backbone,
Cost conscious and determined.

Spring-coiled within her own womb,
Urgently she waits the bursting leaf,
Organising all
And understanding nothing
But the urge to strive.

EIGHT TANKA DANCES

Lake Dance

Sparkles crack the lake;
Creaming over its surface,
Martins toss their wings,
Fold-plunging the milling sky
Midst midge-mingled squalidtudes.

Comb Dance

Scarifying swifts
Knap the air like teasel heads
Hazarding their necks
Against invisible cloth
Crinkle-danced by snagging gnats.

Flower Dance

Boar is a snout-hauled
Missile sundering the glades
With scarlet sunshine;
A turf devouring bristler
Bursting fire from flame red flowers.

Barn Dance

Red bibbed flying fish,
Twitteringly beautiful,
Swallows shoal the barn;
Parasoled by thatch algae,
They challenge the sack corals.

Nest Dance

Arrow apertures
Guarding sandstone battlements:
Exit-entrances
For stage managed sand martins:
These shrines defy defilement.

Card Dance

Biplane dragonfly
Makes a point of making points,
Flipping like a card
Flicked deftly from here to there
By laughing, light-filled fingers.

Wind Dance

Merry wind rider
Armed with a silver head lance,
Rook bucks the wind gusts,
Playing their bunched up rolling
As ripples from a stone drop.

Rook Dance

The child skips for joy
When he sees the shining rooks.
His own black darlings:
He jumps the molehills, laughing,
And plays in the fresh, green grass.

HERB ROBERT

In humus-laden cleft it clings,
This herb on mildewed block;
And, creeping, searches out its path
Across some crannied rock.

With furry stem and ruddy flower
Through algaed stones it weaves
And wanders, whispering its way
Amongst the rotting leaves.

In shady bed, unseen, it sleeps
In pungent ecstasy:
Yet, wide awake, its palmate leaves
Indulge its fantasy.

With penetrating scent it charms
This damp and stony bank;
And flutes a jolly, piping tune
So softly sweet and dank.

All truth is held within its cells;
Here dawns the perfect hour;
The universe is held in thrall;
Herb Robert has the power.

MASK FABLE

There was this man entered a ballroom
He was not wearing a mask
Like everyone else
No one there knew him
He felt like a jackdaw in a garden of peacocks

Lightning flashed
It thundered
The band stopped playing

The masks were angry
Out with him! They cried
He causes a storm

They shot him out like a champagne cork
Their wet exuberance slobbered his shoulders
Shame stripped his self-respect

He was mole
Desperately he tunnelled in the soft earth
Trying to escape

The earth got indigestion
It groaned and heaved heavily
Saying the mole caused it pain
So it spewed him out

It threw him up in a street
Full of masks
Seeing the mole, they gave chase
Unable to run fast

He became an ostrich
Racing across the sand
The masks pursued him on fast horses
Melting away, his legs seeped into the sand.

The masks threw him in a pit
From its edge they glared, mocking him

Lifting him out of the pit, they tortured him
Wear this mask! they said
If you wear this mask you shall have peace

He was scared
He feared pain and death
But he would not wear the mask

He shrunk from their sneers
He cried for mercy
He cringed like a rabbit with a weasel on its back
He wept and they laughed
But they did not destroy him
He was too much of a curiosity

They caged him
All the masks came to see him
He knew he could never wear a mask

There was a great festival
The masks made merry
They danced in the streets
They forgot to lock his cage
He escaped

No one noticed him
They were too preoccupied

The masks went to the ballroom
He decided to follow
Just as he reached it
The earth heaved
Masks lay all over the floor
He danced among them
Like an aspen tree
Like a sea of grass
Like martins over a lake
Like bats in twilight
Like mind across sea

On and on he danced
On through the long night

At dawn he stopped and lifted the masks
From the fallen dancers

Underneath he found nothing
But frightened faces

*

VOICES

I shall marry a maid of France:
We shall live in a pink house
Thatched on the edge of a marsh,
A marsh shaped like a great bowl,
Receiving voices,
The voices of the spheres,
And the songs of Auvergne,
Which are mine and hers
As she sings to me
Beside the marsh
On the estuary
On the edge of the sea.

ECOLOGY

Ploughing four furrows wide and weak
Between the wheat stalks
Tilthing for the weed harvest,
Heedless of the hungry hawk
The urgent man possesses the plains.

Scratching the earth, narrow and strong,
In the open filed,
Working for the wheat harvest,
Famine conscious and hungry,
Hearing the lark sing,
The peasant is the falcon's brother.

Flowers bloom from the boar-rooted soil
Providing bee food
And a ladybird larder,
Granting continuity
And joyous beauty:
The pig is the friend of the primrose.

Butterflies ploughing with bent sticks
Gently scrape the earth,
Communing with working worms
Long after the urgent man
Has departed hence,
Disappearing in a cloud of weeds.

Pigs learnt to plough for butterflies,
Feeding primroses,
Providing bread for the world
And preserving the peasant:
Friends of each other
Before the falcon fell contaminated,
Poisoned by a hoard of urgencies.

Litter

The old lane is littered with paper and tin cans,
Evidencing man's inability to cope:
The mind is troubled and bothered about many things:
If we would make it free, the litter must be moved.

OLD FONSO

Old Alfonso stood
Old Alfonso stood before the door
Old Alfonso stood before

they called his name
to come. Swim, Fonso, swim
(they said) and knew

ninety years were his
at least. His beard was long
and crazy. Slobbed

with hen dung, his boots
clotted the stone path
chunky beside grey flints

winking in the sunlight,
his blue eyes laughing
as bathing boys, clothes

chunked beside pools
loudly called. Beardless
his scythe; barbered now

the dying grass. Brown
his waistcoat, loose
above his sweat-soaked shirt.

Fonso they called him
Fonso they called him then
Fonso they called

before the old church door:
youth-eyed, he thought
sinews were sure. Strength

seemed certain. Endless
were the scything years:
summer soaked the graves'

endless years, their stones
warring, opposed to moss
and burnished blades

and bladed grass, when
Fonso fought the stony fiends,
his enemies, his friends

befriending him with work
to give him purpose – this rooster
crowing in his hen-dunged boots

now standing dead,
dead before the door
of his full church.

JENNY'S BEAUTY

Her beauty is her harmony with life
Before and after all her anguish:
It is her life reflected in her movements,
Telling out the treasures of her thinking;
It is the laughter of her curving lips
Shining bright and showing me her meaning;
It is the language of her moving mind
Turning all her sorrow into pictures
Painted by her heightened understanding,
And forever lifted passed the portal,
Lifted far beyond the bitter choices
Between delight, desire, discipline and duty.

Her beauty is reality enlightened,
Sparkling in her eyes and is not dreaming;
It is the truth of all she is and will be,
Racing tireless, like the sea across the beaches,
And falling like her hair upon her shoulders.

*

STRIVER

There was a man who said:
I'll roll back the sea.
But they mocked him and said:
You can never do such a thing.

He stood on the shore and he said:
You'll never beat me,
I'll roll you back and blow you away
Like the mist in the sky.

The sea roared and heaved,
And he dug in his heels
And he heaved at its leaping form
And lifted it up and he threw
And the sea fell over his arms
And he fell on his face in the sand
With the pain in his heels.

And still he strove with the sea
As it pressed on his head like a cider press
Squeezing his mind and oozing away
The juices of life as he gasped for his breath
Banged flat on the sand
With the pressures of death surging over his head.
He never gave in but fought with the sea
And the sea crushed him flat in the silt of its soul.

And he seized at the sea
And he clutched at the waves and he rolled
And the sea turned him back
And it bashed in his head
And battered him down
With the hammer of time in the surge of the tide.

And it crushed up his bones
And bore him away on the white of its waves,
In the sweep of its troughs,
Like a jelly fish in the swing of the night.

And he mastered the sea as it passed through his cells
In the troughs of his mind in the ocean depths.
He rode on the sea and he rolled it back
As he fathomed its depths and strove no more
To hold in his arms the surge of the tide,
To throw it back and blow it away
Like the mist in the sky.

He entered its mind and he mastered it.
And it rolled with his drift
As he rode on its back.
And rolled it along through the fading night,
Striving no more with the might of the waves,
Merging his mind with the song of the sea,
The master of all as he ceased to strive.

*

The Rook

The trousered rook struts proudly on the bank;
His mate calls harshly to him from their nest;
The railway wagons pass with noisy clank;
Heedless, the rook remains to feed with zest.

His glossy plumage glints with purple sheen;
With wary eye he castes a cheeky look.
This smart young man is very bright and keen;
But is he any happier than the rook?

*

The Road to Castlederg

It's early June on the road to Castlederg:
The curlew calls and the green corn is springing fast:
The turf fire burns and boils the kettle on the hob;
And here laburnum blossom boils in bright cascades.

THE IDLER

He stood, beef-brothed, an idler beside a grey house,
His mind, unwasted in the growing silence,
Travelling through the murky wastes of night.
Uprooted, he stood, freedom flooding his bones;
He smiled faintly;
Sighing, he wondered if the flood were soup
Or inspiration.
He cared neither way:
Soup **is** inspiration to a hungry man.

He was at peace:
Like the drifting moon,
Like the sailing clouds,
Like the flooding soup:
He was the moon, the clouds, the soup:
He was inspiration;
He was the night;
He was the grey house;
He was a blanket;
He was sleep.
But he did not sleep;
He did not go into the house;
He did not go into the house and cover himself with a blanket.
For the house was night and night was a blanket;
The soup was like a warming blanket;
And the soup was inspiration.

>   The clouds were a blanket,
>   And he was the clouds;
>   And so he fed the whole world with soup;
>   He fed the mind of the whole world with inspiration
> soup;
>   He was the mind of the whole world:
>   A child caught up within the cares of time.

*

THE MAGIC SLOT

Like wandering thoughts
Lingering on blown cushions
Leaves fall in the autumn air.

Gusted high upwards
An occasional thought persists
Landing daintily on rough bark,
Caught momentarily
In a magic crevice.

Realisation briefly attained,
It falls, fluttering,
Struggling for freedom,
Falling finally to bed.

Passing through crisp crunchiness
And crackling activity
To restful rustling
Into squelching oblivion,

Feeding the green thoughts of another season
Sun-born to summer glory.

Some, missing the Magic Slot,
Enter a black pond
Choking out their childhood greenery
In despondent croaking.

Polluted frogs croaking for pure air,
Hope for at least one green leaf.

Unslotted thoughts fading in a hungry mind
Sink in the dark pond.

Caught by rough bark,
Only autumn thoughts persist
Knowing all for one second
Before drifting down to renew the fading green leaf,
Fading in spring and knowing nothing,
Fading in its renewal,
Dying in the croak of a polluted frog.

Snatching the falling leaf,
The hand places it in the mind,
Freeing the frog and fixing it in the Magic Slot.

*

THE BANQUET

A laughter-hollowed grey mouth
Engulfing the flames of joy
Crunches the fire seed
Mockingly between two bulldozers
Smoothing the dying embers.

The laughter gloats in relief
Through the fearful hall
Furnished by vanquished servants
Greed ridden and starved
By the scraping bulldozers
Creating wealth for the fearful gibberers,

Who become grey islands in a sea of fire
Forgetting they were once a great mouth
Gloating fearfully in their gardens
Laid out in the hollow hall,
Bathed complacently in princely praise
Mocking, leeringly, the master's man.

Fire-churned guts blast the mouth-roof.
Splitting it like heated rocks.
The hollow mockers
Are scattered like clouds in a blazing sunburst,
Like sparks from a blazing fire,
Like mocking laughter in an echo,
Like a gibbering, grey mouth
In a sweat-crazed blaze of belly-burst.

*

COMIC VERSE AND WORSE

Smelly Ellie

The fart of a man is bad enough,
The fart of a dog is worse;
But the fart from the arse of an elephant bull
Makes even an angel curse.

The thunderous noise from the thick black clouds
As they roll across the skies
Is nothing compared with the sound that comes
From between his massive thighs.

The smell from a thousand sewers at once
Will waft on the wind and fade;
But, try as you might, you will never remove
The stench that his arse has made.

Purposeful Witch

Luscious, young de-knickered dame
Lying low in lust-lined frame,
Sighing now that you are spent:
No use asking where it went.

Black and white, you played your card,
Making sure it would be hard:
Indeed, 'twas better that way so:
Dangling dicks will never do.

Stronger none than your prim spell,
Working out your purpose well:
Better than the bat's blood lark;
Yours will raise a second spark.

Skylarking with P B Shelly

Hail to thee blithe streaker,
        Man thou never wert:
Thou art a maiden stripper
        Practising her art,
Who dost let fly an unpremeditated fart

FOUR TANKA TRUTHS

Helmingham

The old meadow oak
Frames in its dying branches
A distant pink house:
Rooks, in turmoil, stir the sky;
Primroses bloom in the woods.

Tea

Let your mind go free;
See the ashwood burning bright;
Slowly sip your tea:
In the stillness of the night
Drinking tea is such delight.

Truth

Buddha is dried dung:
Knowing the unknowable
Is to look within.
Why look to the infinite
When the truth is at your feet?

God

God is an oak tree
Living, growing and dying,
Never eternal;
Providing a home for all;
Sustaining, not creating.

MEMORIES

The toothless old man sits
Nonchalantly dipping his biscuit
Into his tea
As he gazes inconsequentially out
Over the curvaceous sea.
Tea in clustered droplets
Bedews his drooping moustaches
As his mind falls far and fast,
Through circuitous mists and dew-bedraggled dawns,
Into a distant past.

SEVEN HAIKU

The dog's nose is cold;
He sits in front of the fire;
The fire is dying.

Hoof marks in the mud
Along the pine-scented lane:
The forge walls are wet.

Old branches creaking
In the dark woods as goldcrests
Twitter in the leaves.

The shining, sharp spade
Slices through the frozen clods
In the cold, crisp air.

Pigs root for acorns;
There is a smell of dank leaves,
And noisy munching.

At the minster door
The pilgrim rests his tired feet
And the priest falls down.

Enveloping fog,
Overwhelmingly gentle:
Suddenly, a crash.

SHADOW WISDOM

Emerging from the shadows, rise and shake
Enlightenment before the eyes of men;
Reveal to them the panther's rump and rake
Each one's desire to lie within your den.
There coax them forth to fertilise the earth
And bring release to all who come to you
With burdens seeming greater than life's worth
Until you mingle them with dust and dew.

MOTHER GODDESS

Come Mother of all reason and repose,
Enclose your children safe within your breast!
Yours is the balance, yours the realm that knows
No conflict, opposites, no pain, no quest
For answers, resolutions, antidotes
For wrongly minded thoughts of how things are
Or were or will be; no discordant notes
Deter, no absolutes are there to mar
The oneness of all things in life, in death;
And even there are not apart; they're one
Within the advent of exhaling breath
Where void is substance and the substance done,
> As gone, we come, we climb beyond the tomb
> To rest once more within our Mother's Womb.

STONE AGE

When metal replaced stone the mind withered;
People could no longer transmit their thoughts;
Air became a barrier to them all;
Outer power took over from the inner;
Thrusting acquisition split the womb's hold,
Placing artefacts above discernment,
Until metal towers and tiny chips usurped
Our mindful hold upon the universe.

Silly Women

Thinking to reach the mountain peak,
Silly women throw their legs wide
Only to be pierced by its point.
Many boulders, bursting from their wombs,
Bounce far and wide, but some remain,
Sons of their preserving instinct,
Move hoards of misery forest-ward.
There's comfort here. No loveless lust
Shall stifle Mother Earth's goodwill.
She shall bring forth a leveller
Who, riding out, shall overthrow
The biders from their glory seats,
And rise to govern in their stead.

BETRAYAL

A hunter brave without a care
Took up his bow and shot a hare.
He built a fire and, on a spit,
He turned it round and roasted it.

With sizzling flesh and burning eyes
The carcase filled the air with sighs;
Why have you played this dirty trick
And pierced my innards with a stick?

He gave the spit another turn:
What was there here for him to learn?
You are not mine; we are not wed;
You never came to share my bed.

I took you in; you shared my life;
I would have been your own true wife;
You turned me out and made me run,
Then arrowed me for food and fun.

Release

Go forth into the night to find the day;
Depart, return; there is no other way;
Accept what is as part of what shall be
And was. The endless end evaporates, is free
From nothingness, from form, from clinging on
To aimless thoughts, to all that's come and gone.

Undaunted

See how the maze shall wend
      Passed all deceivers;
See how it shall defend
      All true believers!
Unwind the ball of twine
      Tread forth undaunted;
All power shall hold the line
      Where truth is flaunted.

Love's Long Home

Sickle left among the wheat,
Poppies blooming at his feet,
There he lay entwined in red
Waiting for the marriage bed.

Maiden, would you come this way?
Would you wed with him this day?
No indeed, not on a farm
Where the poppies come to harm.

See his sickle laid aside!
Is the gap not very wide?
Maybe yes, but in the corn
Babes of mine must not be born.

Turning from the rich, red earth,
Shall he leave his land of birth?
Yes, indeed, and wed to me,
Evermore he shall be free.

Blown away, as if like dust,
Freedom's life depends on trust.
Trust my thighs and trust my womb;
Trust the thrust of love's long home.

SONG AND DANCE

There's got to be a song in all we say;
A melody set to the tune of time:
There's got to be a dance in all we do:
A rhythmic movement in the mode of mime.

There's got to be some music in our hands,
In the way we teach our fingers how to sing:
There's got to be some dancing in our speech
To make it sparkle like a diamond ring.

There's a tune for every phase upon the way;
We must learn to feel the rhythm in the rain,
To hear the music in the dancing eyes,
To write a poem for every cry of pain.

ANOTHER WORLD

Another world lies far beyond this gate
Through templed avenues of towering trees,
Through coiffured tresses of a courtly dame
Who cannot walk along the paths I tread.
She sees them only from her castle wall.
She's soon offended if I stroke her hair;
She fails to understand the woodland ways;
She cannot feel affection in the leaves
Or hear the silence in the moaning wind:
She sees no love at all in furry mice
Or wisdom in the raven's croaking call.
I look as through a window at this dame
(Who will not walk along the paths I tread)
An oak framed window in the woodland wall,
The brickless wall that runs the whole world round,
The wall that forms a barrier to some,
And yet is there and must be breached by those
Who would make sense of every mouse's squeak
And see the dainty dancing of the bee.
Perhaps she works within her castle walls
Some mystery I'll never understand;
Some game that I can never learn to play,
Equipping her to face the trials of time
Far better than my world can do for me.
But I would never change the walless wall
For anything within her castle tower:
I'd rather die within the bounds of truth
Than live in fear equipped to conquer all.

Promise

The weeds of today are the flowers of tomorrow;
The joy that we have is the child of our sorrow.

The rays of warm sunshine rain showers on the forest;
The seeds on the shop shelf are flowers to the florist.

The words in the bright eyes need never be spoken;
The fine china tea cup need never be broken.
*

Reconciliation

See when passing fields,
Standing there beneath the trees,
Tail-swishing horses
Reconciled, except for flies,
To everything around them.

Standing in the market see
Around you people
Sweating in the heat of day,
Giving and receiving pay,
Swearing and grasping,
Reconciled to nothing save
The foul flies filthy laughter.

Industrial Relations

Who are the management and who the workers?
Where do we find the men and where the shirkers?

One blames the other, stating this and that,
Whilst, on the proceeds, rogues grow rich and fat.

Co-operation seems the way to gain;
To do it any other way's insane.

KINDLY ANIMALS

The warm and furry mammal folk,
They feed their young on milk:
The kindly hearted crocodile,
He clothes his son in silk.

The wise and noble mammal folk,
They teach their young their steps:
I wish the reptiles weren't so kind
And fed their young on reps.

*

BUFFALO GOOSE

Necks stretching into tomorrow, geese fly,
Heads skeining ahead of body needs,
Pulling plummet pots propelled by looping wings
Warming to wetlands as curving buffalo horns.

Like horns half-blown by inexperience,
Wire-whining wings foretell their flight-path
Arrowing across the avid autumn skies
Greedy for the coming winter snows.

Gaggling loose over open hinterland,
Inquisitors potentially long-lived,
Accomplishing tasks beyond the scope of bellied-buffalo,
Geese glean the last secrets from the stubbled fields.

What secrets then has this old gander
Who, they say, has visited here these twenty years or more?
He's seen some ice-bound polar bears near Spitzbergen
Perhaps musk oxen also; but never a buffalo.

Why then are geese and buffalo so inter-twined?
In differing ways they both enfold the earth
Between the leaf and fresh, life-bringing breeze,
Binding all beyond the setting sun to rise perpetual.

*

ART GIRL

Why she studies work
Is beyond comprehension.
She was born for art:
A water droplet leaping
High to sculpt the beetling rock.

SHE AND ME

Here within this room
I beheld the universe:
Tinted, vibrant, bright,
Moving timeless, a capsule
Encompassing everything.

IS

Emerging from the night, she sped towards me.
Stopped. I opened the door. She entered.
Her cry came to me as the chough calling above the cliffs.
The red of her lips was as the thread of life along the seashore.
Folding me in her wings, she bore me out over the sea.
We lay together on an island fingered by the waves' reach.
Whispering among the rocks, they taught me how to search into her being.

Holding me between her thighs, she lifted me.
I saw the reason for night.
It was her womb.
Issuing from it, I took up my brush and painted her eyes into the beginning of a new day.
She was called IS and, without her, nothing ever was that is.

Rhinomouse

I am Rhinomouse:
I mind a herd of industrious cows
Gold-lining their udders
With rich croppings from wealth-managed pastures.
Princesses of fortune,
They pity my penniless state.
They are mistaken.
They are replaceable.
I am not.

SYNTHESIS

Her searching tongue seeks out the flow of moon and milk:
She flicks it round the poignancy of sap-seeped night,
That drenches her before the lake's wide dishpan-hold
Can shorten distance through the misting dress
Exposing wanton thighs beneath a leaf-capped lust to be
At one with fluxing time's uncertain hold on life.

Only when her tongue holds still is mind released
And time is seen as just another part of all,
Controlled by thighs that grip the rocket blasting purpose
In the tenderness of things, directing it
To charge the universal womb of synthesis
Between the fall of milk-fed night and timelessness.

REALITY

Beneath a bright laburnum tree in early June,
Golden-haired and wearing a green dress,
The Goose Girl sat alone
Gazing at her grazing geese across the plain,
When, playing on a flute and dressed in russet brown,
There came that way a peasant lad
Who asked the girl her name
And why she was so pensive sitting there,
Her shoulders coloured yellow
In a flow of falling gold.

Beneath his shock of tumbling hair
The peasant's eyes were burning bright
On hearing this and so he asked:
What lucky man is this?
What is his name and who is he
That here does leave so sweet a girl
Alone upon this sweeping plain?

I call my man Reality:
He does not leave me;
Here he is beside me now upon this bank;
By day he roots himself into the ground,
Becoming here this bright laburnum bush.

Where is the truth in what you say?
Your lover a laburnum bush?
For sure I know this cannot be;
What proof have you that such a thing exists?

Wait here and watch the fall of night
When, in the twilight gap, he'll change
And drive with me the geese across the plain.

The peasant waited, hiding in a nook,
Concealed behind an oak tree's gnarled defence;
But in the falling dusk the bush remained,
Leaving the girl alone to drive her geese to rest
Across the rolling plain.

Upon the day that followed
Once again the peasant came to see
The maiden seated there beneath the burning blooms
Cascading golden yellow in the sun.

You lied to me;
You never told me true;
Your lover's no laburnum bush;
It never stirred;
He never helped you drive the geese to rest;
You have no lover;
That, for sure, I know;
Unless he's something else
Besides this cursed laburnum bush.

Lifting high her head, the Goose Girl shook her golden hair,
Laughing bright as sunlight with her eyes:
You failed to see because your eyes were blind.
His spirit left the bush and came with me,
Taking on a handsome prince's form.
Tonight, bestir yourself and turn your steps

Towards the cottage in the dell
And there look in the window when I light the lamp
And see there, for yourself, Reality.

That night the peasant made all hast
And found the lighted cottage in the dell,
Its window sparkling brightness through the trees.
He looked within and there saw such a sight
His heart beat faster than the speedy notes
He often played upon his tuneful flute.
The girl performed a scintillating dance
The like of which he'd never seen before.
Her hands were singing to her body's tune,
Conducted by her deftly dancing feet
That matched the swinging rhythm of her hips.
She was a fairy orchestra conducted
By the twirling of her dress
That presently began to twirl so fast
If fell around her feet,
Like grass before a mower's swinging scythe,
Revealing fast an undulating lawn of grassless beauty.

*

Moving her shining body into shade,
She donned a rose-red robe
More delicate in colour than the dawn,
And putting out the light,
Went through a door into another room.

The peasant swooned and fell among the ferns
And sleeping in the June night's balmy air,
Saw not the Goose Girl's man Reality.
Awaking with the dawn, he stole away

To wait beside the gold laburnum tree
Where, when the Goose Girl came behind her geese,
He bitterly accosted her.
Complaining that she'd played him false again.

Play me false once more
And I shall take may sharpest axe
And fell this cursed laburnum bush:
Where then shall be your man Reality?

The Goose Girl laughed and tossed her golden hair;
You know full well you'd never touch the bush,
For you desire too much to meet reality.

That night the peasant came much later
To the maiden's cottage in the dell
And went behind and peered into the window there
And saw her clad again in her red robe
Preparing at the fire a tasty meal.
She laid two places on the white
And well emaciated table top
Scrubbed cleaner than a freshly opened flower.
Then, smiling spells out from her magic teeth,
The goose girl softly called.
And coming through an inner door,
A handsome prince appeared
Arrayed in green and golden robes
And took the red-robed girl into his arms.
Caring not to see much more of this,
The peasant fled out fast into the night,
His heart low sinking in despair
That such a thing, in fact, could ever be.

Upon the morrow it was growing dusk
Before he came again across the plain
To seek fair Duty seated there beneath her tree.
She wasn't there, but driving at that hour
Her geese before her to the dell.
On seeing him she called for him
To come and help her drive the geese
And learn at last the truth about her man Reality.

Last night I saw him in your room
And never wish to see him more :
He's no friend of mine who dares to love
The fairest maid upon the plains.

Duty laughed like tinkling bells across the plain.
You never did see such a man within my room.
Reality was never there last night:
You did but see the mist of your imaginings.
Now come with me and sit down for a meal
And I will show you my Reality.
You'll not dislike him that for sure I know.

Reluctantly the peasant helped to drive the geese
And entered then the cottage in the dell,
Where once again fair Duty danced for him
Her twirling, tempting dance.
And when at last she called him to the meal,
He was surprised to see two places only laid.
Duty beamed at him a pearly smile:
Sit down, my man, and take your rightful place with me.
The peasant sighed and knew at last Reality.

THE ABBOT

There came this abbot
Contemplating life's purpose
Before the altar:
Where once despair reigned supreme,
One meagre light now brings hope.

SHE-WOLF RIDING HOOD

That day in the park they said that here
Was hotter than it was in Barcelona;
And the Red Riding Hood Wolf-Dog smiled roguishly
Through the eyes of his willow-clad mistress
As a last philosophical swallow
Edged its innocence between October leaves.

On the chance of a chill dawn,
The swallow dips his chin and travels south
And leaves the girl to carry sunshine
To her wolf-warm bed where rod iron rays
Bisect the planetoidal curves of Quest
And carve a kingdom for returning spring.

In June, when swallows hatch their young,
The wolf-tongue searches out sharp pinnacles of pain
As newborn cries tell out a man-child's birth,
All because on that October day
Not even Barcelona was as hot as were
The she-wolf eyes inside Red Riding Hood.

LATE MAY DREAMS

Taciturn,
Lolling hemlock flops,
Paunching the ditches in the shimmering sunlight.

Fortuitous in the face of fear,
Somnambulant heads nod derision,
Filling sewers with the scent of sheep's parsley.

Smutting the umbelliferous waves
With multitudinous dots,
Black flecks determine
Afternoon slumbers
Longing for activity
Leaning over the gate in the late
May evening falling through
The tall elms
Topping the rise at the end of the wandering day.

DOG SUBSTITUTE

My girl is a dog substitute.
When she dances, I leap round her
Like a bouncing ball. She catches me,
Chews, then tosses me up for more.

My little bitch died of old age.
No longer does she night-nuzzle
Reality into my dreams.
Trust is replaced by plush buttocks.

Where paws once implored attention
Subterfuge undermines my need,
Activating a cavern
Of contrived necessity.

Kisses, manipulated by giggles,
Delay sleep and substitute mirrors
For the warm tongue unbunging
The glad bottles of resourceful night.

Whereas I once controlled wag-tailed games
Over clutching tufts of grass,
Today I've become a game
Where grass slithers under bare-backed ridicule.

THE CREATOR

They brought him this block of stone
and they said: carve a man
for the midst of our town;
and he sat in front of the block
many hours and he looked
till his mind was a blank;
and he leapt to his feet
and called for his dog
and went for a walk in the park
that were stocky with oaks.

And he came to that block every day
and gazed deep down to its depths
till his eyes became sore
like the sides of an unwatered tank;
and they hurried him up;
for the time that the statue was needed
was near and they placed in his hands
the hammer and chisel for him to begin;
and he chipped away at the block
till a stone man appeared,
at which they all gasped and cried:
he's real, just like one of us and superb.

But he sat in front of the man
and he watched him for hours
till his mind made a blank
and he called for his dog
and he walked in the woods

that were stocky with oaks
and he smelt of their essence
and he savoured the shape of their trunks
and heard the whispering truth
of their wavy-edged leaves.

And he ran from the woods
and took up the heaviest hammer
he had in the house and smote
to the earth the silken-faced statue
of stone and struck it to bits
till only a jagged, irregular lump
remained in the midst of the granules
and choking white dust.

And he took up the lump
and sat it up here
in the midst of the town
and he said, behold my creation,
the work of my hands untaught
by the needs of a populace
lusting for power
and copied from nothing at all
save the hewing of wood
in the heat of the conflict
deep in the striving
energy bank of my brain.
And they all stood amazed

at the wrath of his presence,
but scorned the work of his hands
until they beheld the glint of the stone
and the thousands of shapes
that it had when viewed from
as many angles as ever there were.

Their amazement was turned into awe
and they fell down and worshipped
the man who dared to create
from the heat of his brain
this thing that the like of
had never been seen since
the urge to create had first
overcome the copyist's craft.

And he walked with his dog
through the oaks
and he worshipped their power.

HOUSE SPARROW

Neat capped and smart, he sits supreme,
Roof-lord and law dispenser,
Himself governed by bill-enforced
Laws. A licensed rogue before

His own house door, his squatter's rights
Ensuring his domicile there,
His family secure beneath the eaves:
Prestigious fellow, inclined to advertise

His controversial presence,
Sure to stimulate annoyance or
Enjoyment. This sleek-suited bouncer
Exploits situations. Relentlessly

Persistent in endeavour as a tycoon
Pursuing wealth. Neater in execution,
Less particular of offensiveness and
Blest by wasteful indifference,

He waxes bold on boughs and tall pots
Waiting his chance to rob and plunder,
Chattering brittle defiance. Inscrutable,
Resilient in mind, a master robber

And trained technician. Adaptable
To tit tactics on feeders. Using
All resources to advantage,
Consolidating his world in man's

And all but mastering him, playing
On his guilt complex and indifference,
Multiplying in the shade of his cupidity;
Chirping his sleek power in red-roofed affluence.

He reigns supreme.

SECRETARY BEAR

This secretary is a teddy bear:
Her hug-ability persists
On park seats, computers
And the occasional night out.

She tips her bowl of audacious growls
Into the office tureen,
Where the mirth of her middle-aged licence
Soups up managerial oats
With the bashed onions
Of worker frustration.

LIFE IS A FRUIT CAKE

Thoughtfully the boy negotiates
the cliff of cake whose crumbling pieces
are disintegrating clods and rocks.

Seabirds are the voices leaping from
his urgent eyes as fingers reach
for flight above the mind's dark precipice.

Currents carry fish to feed
the wistful guillemots that motion-leaf
the jagged tangibility of grumbling rocks.

Whiskered shrimps are savoured on the tongue
as raisins grit his teeth and gannets slit
the empty plate like knives through milk.

Now is every day laid at his feet;
for he has seen a lifetime pass
in minutes whilst a plum cake disappeared.

*

THE CARRION CROW

Look! The carrion crow
in the park is carcase prone,
jerking out benevolence
with wit to bless us

and our ways with plops
of slow determined pulp,
that tone the vegetation's
long considered death.

before he lifts his bill
preparing to conduct
his humping chorus voice
to stardom in a rowan bush.

His grandpa's purse is sewn
close with beady glints
that sight no obvious paths
leading to confidence.

beware he does not double up
deceive by hop and crop
across this soggy leisure place
poorer by half without his stop,

that twinkles twenty times and beats
considered efforts to improve
the beauty that so many
artificially desire to have.

His is the artifice
of duty that designs
unhindered by the preconceived.
His harshness edifies

just as a chopping axe
can place a pulse in wooden blocks.
He's the structure with the ploy
that swings his cracking pluck

to mace the sluggish park
with vibrant scenes on carcase tops
far grander in their powerful sets
than all these neatly planted plots.

*

The Turn of the Tide

They taught me the truth at the turn of the tide;
They taught me the truth it is true;
But what they had taught me was not what they thought;
And they never knew how I knew.

They knew that I knew; they knew that I cared;
They knew that I knew that they knew;
But they never learned how the cakes were burned
In the fall of the morning dew.

They stood with me by the side of the sea;
But they neither saw nor heard:
They never did learn what the sea had to say,
And they missed the flight of the bird.

They could not tell as they stood in the wood
Why the tree had grown so tall;
They never did find who cut through the mind
On the day they saw it fall.

They sat with me at the ebb of the tide,
To meditate in the dark,
But they never found out who gave the shout
When the arrow found its mark.

They came with me to the flow of the tide,
And they tried to give me a chance:
They thought they knew what was good and true,
But I only wanted to dance.

They taught me the truth at the turn of the tide;
They taught me the truth that I knew;
That I knew all along what the truth had been;
That I knew what it was to be true.

*

SIGHTLESS VISION

There is an inner seeing without sight,
A seeing in the darkness of the mind,
A darkness no more evil than the light,
A brightness from the blackness of the blind.

In peaceful sleep along the shades of night,
Secure as rests the infant in the womb,
In den of darkness, soothing sweet delight,
We find a friend as lasting as the tomb.

The light alone is vastly incomplete;
It strikes no path along the middle way:
Without the darkness it can never meet
The needs of man or hold his fears at bay.

A darkless god is like a rootless tree,
Whose leaves take light, but cannot use its power:
Such useless, unreal gods can never be;
The mayfly shows us more in just one hour.

The path to truth lies not with gods or men:
It is both here in darkness and in light;
It is the gentle voice that whispers: when?
The song of sunshine and the hymn of night.

No Escape

Anger in the heart:
Is there no escape from it?
Seek not to escape:
Let the rain fall on your face;
Let it gently caress you.

Hatred in the mind:
Is there no escape from it?
Seek not to escape:
Let the breeze blow on your cheek
Bringing the scent of jasmine.

Are the thoughts bitter?
Is there no escape from them?
Seek not to escape:
Listen to the thrush singing:
Smell the primrose on the path.

CHINESE POEMS

LIFE
The wheelwright works in wood: ash, oak and elm:
Each with its own soft smell and textured grain:
The cart horse pulls the wagon in his wake;
The smell of horse and wood is life itself.

LITTER
The old lane is littered with paper and tin cans,
Evidencing man's inability to cope:
The mind is troubled and bothered about many things:
If we would make it free, the litter must be moved.

TENDERNESS
The small child toddles along the path;
He rejoices in the bright sunshine.
The fresh leaves on the trees are tender;
The child's feet are soft and tender too.

NOTHING ABIDES
The forest god sits in a tall oak;
The leaves hide him from the gaze of men:
A stream flows, bubbling, through the green woods:
The god's hair flows over the branches.

RENDING
The sleek cat sits proudly on the chair
Smoothing his whiskers with his grey paws:
A pretty girl tears men with her smile:
The cat tears his prey with his strong claws.

THE SINKING HEART

The roding woodcock flies his course at dusk
Through the still air beside the forest edge:
The sinking heart beats slow and stops in death;
The woodcock sinks and rests beneath the oaks.

I WENT UP TO MANCHESTER

I went up to Manchester, a hundred miles across;
Manchester came down to me and said: I'll be your boss.

She built for me a cotton tower ten thousand metres tall;
I sat upon its pinnacle and watched her workers crawl.

She dug for me a cavern ten miles beneath the earth;
I stored within its emptiness her wealth for what its worth.

She dashed some soot into my face and sent me straight to hell;
I bounced right back up again and gave a mighty yell.

I picked her up and swung her round and threw her in the sea;
Within the hole she left behind there grew a mighty tree.

I climbed into its branches and swung upon its boughs;
It dropped ten billion acorns to feed a million sows.

All the birds in heaven were there; they built them leafy nests;
And no one came to bother them or call them little pests.

MOON DANCE

Moon in the belly, moon in the heart,
Moon drifting with us right from the start,
Making an effort, tripping along,
Teaching us calmly how to belong,
Softly she shades us, gleaming she goes,
Gliding us swiftly out on our toes.
Beauty of star-shine, Goddess of Night,
Queen of the Shades, entwining twilight,
She knows the purpose, reason and hour
For making dragons, giving them power,
Guiding them sure-foot, skipping in fun,
Sending them dancing, making them one,
Not with the darkness, not with the day,
But with the shade-time ever to stay.
Shade-time is moon time, not a jot more,
Weaving its patterns, pictures galore.
Mother of dragons, huntress supreme,
Merge now our realness into your dream.

Broody Goose

On leaving her nest
the broody goose envelopes
her eggs in soft down.
She murmurs over the grass,
grazing like a gurgling pot

seeking to subdue
exultant honks. She hisses
at a hunting cat,
whose surprise-wide eyes erupt
to leap its lives to safety.

The nest has six eggs
with one oval and warm stone
to make seven.
The goose returns, nestling in
like a boat in foamy seas.

Less lofty than swans
and wiser in adaption,
she sees off beasts and
strangers, but welcomes all the
food and water that I bring

They say seven geese
eat as much grass as one cow.
I kike this great bird
better than swans, cows and ducks:
her style is stauncher than theirs.

*

Belonging

Beyond is far away and yet is near;
In silent voice it lifts us far above
The foibles of disquietude and brings
Us home to rest awhile where no pain moves.

Belonging is beyond and yet is here:
With sightless eyes it sees us safely through
The pulsing trammels of desire until
We reach the fullness of our emptiness.

Such emptiness masks everything but truth:
Its soundless sound belies its pregnant form,
Which holds the all in thrall to mindfulness
Until we, freed, belong beyond recall.

WOLF FIRE

Flames fluctuating, fire fascinates us.
Tonguing, tortuously between laid logs,
Wandering wolf-like, warily it tracks,
Tacking in search of sustaining substance.
Biting bare to the bone, wolves create logs,
Licking them clean with fire-like precision,
Paws pressing hard as jaws crumble and crunch,
Reaching the marrow and creating embers
Endlessly in the struggle to survive.
Wolves weave their way across the northern wastes;
Pruning out the weak and weary, fire-like,
Their jaws, tongues and teeth cleanse all around them.

*

LAMMAS

The rotund richness of the ripening corn
Delivers up the Goddess to her fate,
Befalling her to favours long since formed
With the welcome of her winsomeness,
As, aging now, her matron-mantle moves
To cover her in comely counterpoint.
A mass of melodies combine to form
The comfort of her nature-laden cloak,
So soon to feed the hunger of her brood
Begotten of her changing attitudes.
In twining twilight now she twists her way,
Defiant as the daring bats' delight
In bearing back to bank and catch their prey,
Predominant within the shifting shades.
She shifts, she moves, she changes all the while,
And yet abides, unchanging, with us all.
We recognise her not, but she is here
And there and everywhere, as is the corn
That symbolises all her caring ways.
Unfettered in her praise, both night and day,
Arise, delight and dance the Goddess-way!

INTER-DEPENDENCE

Lilting and laughing and longing for love,
Dancing, we drift with the cooing grey dove.
Craftily caring, we hunt with the hawk,
Heeding its hunger, we steal up and stalk,
Stealthily hoping the two of us meet,
Feeder and feeding to rest at our feet.
Watching and waiting, in life and in death,
Feeds one the other and gives them both breath.
Captive and caring and kind, it's the key,
Latching and loosing, that sets us all free.
Touching and taking, united in love,
Feeding the falcon, we drift with the dove.

*

MIDSUMMER'S DAY

Winding here and wending there,
Dragon Dill shall now appear:
Over hill and over dale,
Fear you not that he will fail.
Follow him in loud full cry,
Let him teach us how to try
All and every way to find
Ways of learning to be kind.
Twisting high and twisting low,
Let him teach us how to show
Up and down to be but one.
Let the earth go round the sun,
Let the seasons move around,
Let us make a merry sound;
Wholesome, fruitful, let them come,
Winsome, snow-full, beat the drum;
Changing ever, let them pass.
Skip we now across the grass,
Dancing through the longest day,
Letting Summer have her say.

HELMINGHAM

Return to me before the memory fades,
Before the falling of the autumn leaves,
To touch them as they turn from green to red
Revealing their full brilliance in decay.

Return to me before you too are dead,
Before the swallows fly beyond the bar
To cross the seas, the deserts, winging out
Beyond the opposites of near and far.

Return to me as now I turn to you
For one last time before this mound of truth,
As Helm once stood to beckon us to dance,
Entwined, beyond the realms of life and death.

*

INTER-RELATIONSHP

My thoughts reach out beyond the universe,
And yet remain unknown to those around,
Unless, at times, I choose to loose them forth
In speech to those of whom I think should hear
And understand what I suppose I know.
To know and not to know, each are the same;
We do but tap into the theme of things,
And know without the wisdom of the spheres.
If I, when others speak of me, should heed
Their every word, what good should come of it
Unless the wise prevail above the known?
And why should I suppose I know the best,
Or better than the most of what I hear?
Do I create my thoughts, or have they come
To me from outer space? Not one is mine,
And yet I own the universe. Not this;
For what owns me, I own within myself:
The One owns All, and so the All owns One;
For Wisdom's wisest Way is infinite
In one relationship through everything.

SNOWED IN

Messenger of sleep, the staunch snow falls,
Blanketing our dreams with flakes of truth.
Darkness daunts not where the whiteness lies
Daring us to break death's barriers.

Snuggle down beneath the cold and wait,
Where disaster, frigid fathoms deep,
Fearfully dispenses with the truth,
Pushed aside, betrayed, within our thoughts.

Cold disaster threatens, endless, vast,
Causing us to bungle and mistrust:
Faithful to the obvious we fall,
Heedless of the staunch and friendly snow.

Good and evil are but opposites,
Figments of the mind, explaining all,
Save how each drifting flake disperses
All into the oneness of its wonderment.

OLD ALICE

I always associate wood smoke
with aprons, Old Alice and the globe
artichokes along her garden wall.

She used to light fires for all seasons:
artichoke heads peered above the sliceable
blobs of sap-spewed summer smoke.

Gold ear rings escorted her gap-grin
as she watched me chew up buttered
artichokes tasting of smoke-soaked apron.

During autumn her fires grew misty
with sprites wisping up from thistle-crackling
artichoke stems and brittle leaves.

In winter she wore a black apron
and appeared footless as she glided,
stoking the globulous glow of her bonfire.

Her spring fires were a revelation:
sparks sped smokeless and new artichokes
clustered in the crumble of wood ash.

Now Alice is dead and raspberries
grow where her artichokes used to burst
from the fertile flames of all seasons.

*

FEBRUARY FEARS

A million autumn seeds are dying
in this fungal bed of February fears,
volcanoed by these moss-encrusted stumps
and algaed stems,
as others strive to germinate,
uncertain as a doubting horse before a jump,
protesting fading ploys
against the spring's
disputed, long delayed debut.

This catkinned hazel copse
Belies its beauty,
Unrevealed to undiscerning eyes,
Who, anxious only for the green-backed pound,
Are living on their February fears.

COURAGE

Courage is not the prerogative of
The holder of medals or of the soldier:
Courage is the tender leaf in spring
Bursting from its bud into the frosty air:
It's the blade of grass struggling to pierce
The drought ridden earth.

Courage is the mother hen defending
Her chicks from the marauding cat; and then
It's the boy climbing in the tall tree,
Or, when at school, he faces the cruel bully.
Courage is the essence of existence,
The mantle of the seeker after truth.

*

JENNY

Many were the mindful moments,
Happy were the passing days,
When my love was there beside me
Walking down the silken ways.

Bright her hair beside the briars
Smiling at the ripening hips;
Clinging were her wisping tresses
Blowing round her rosy lips.

Bright her smile as sparkling sunshine:
Quick she stepped and skipped along
Holding tight my hand but gently,
Laughing in each step a song.

Hers the cares and hers the sorrows,
Hers the stabs that never die,
Grasping as a bramble thicket
Buried in her bosom lie.

Hers the love that never questions,
Hers the love that never dies,
Giving all and never doubting
Warming when the west wind sighs.

Teaching me the joyful pathways
She forever gave me peace;
Resting 'neath the golden archways,
From the pain she brought release.

Like the rain upon the window
Dripping from the dying leaf;
Like the whispers in the west wind,
Like the binding of the sheaf.

These were hers and mine together,
Ours and ours alone to see,
Shared forever in the forest
Lying 'neath the linden tree.

*

NO ONE DIED FOR ME

No one died especially for me;
For death brings life to all,
And all must die,
And all must die for all,
Just as a tree's own leaves die and decay
Upon the woodland floor
Bringing sustenance to that which gave them birth.

What greater miracle is there than this:
That all sustains the all,
And all must live,
And all must live for all,
Just as when a flock of rooks fly out
To feed in open fields,
They post them sentinels to warn of danger?

THE MERRY SOW

A big fat sow lived wild and free
Aroving in the shady woods:
She dug a hole beneath a tree
And in it stored her worldly goods.

Upon her head she wore a hat
As red as was her hide as black:
She said her prayers upon a mat,
And gathered acorns in a sack.

She worshipped at the shrine of Boar,
Who gave her strength to root about
Amongst the leaves on forest floor
To dig out truffles with her snout.

She wore a red and yellow smock,
In which she used to dance a jig
Upon a tall and noble rock:
She was a truly merry pig.

*

THE COMMON SUNFLOWER

The common sunflower grows up tall
And never seems to mind at all
When little mice run up its stalk
And sit upon its leaves to talk.

After a time its head bows down,
And in the sun it turns quite brown.
When hungry mice run up to feed
Gives them all its oily seed.

It gives them all excepting one
Which grows especially ripe in sun,
And falling down on fertile soil,
It lies for months preserved in oil.

The frosts of winter bury it,
Protecting it from hungry tit;
And when the springtime comes again,
It sends out roots in warming rain.

In summertime it grows up tall
And does not seem to mind at all
When little mice run up its stalk
To sit upon its leaves and talk.

Handmaidens

The pope has twelve nuns:
One bakes his buns;
One irons his sheet;
One massages his feet;
One cooks his lunch;
Another has a hunch;
One washes his vestments;
One makes his investments;
One winds up his clocks;
One darns his socks
One attends mass;
One grooms his ass;
What of the last one?
She's there just for fun.

A HORSE CALLED PUNCH

Wandwyn had been left a small farm, but he had no money to buy a plough and a horse to pull it. Having to do all the work by hand meant that he was unable to cultivate enough land to ensure his prosperity.

One day, as he was wandering over the moors wondering if he should sell the farm, he heard a melodious voice that filled him with a strange yearning. Glancing around him, he presently beheld a girl in a knee-length, russet-coloured dress sitting on a knoll combing her hair and singing. Familiar with the moor as he was, he was surprised he had never before come across this hillock. It began to rain. Walking up to the girl, he asked if it bothered her.

'Why no,' she retorted, flashing him a pearly smile. 'It cools me away from the heat of the fire.'

'The fire?'

'Why yes. In the forge,' she stamped her foot on the knoll. 'In here. My father's the blacksmith.'

Wandwyn sniffed. The smell of burning hoof was unmistakable. Looking down the far side of the knoll, he could see a powerfully built, bearded man shoeing a horse in a forge built into the hillside. 'I could do with a horse like that,' he said.

The girl laughed. 'Desire it enough and you shall have it.'

'Rosina! Rosina!' the smith called. 'Where are you? Come and bring me some ale.'

Jumping up, the girl ran down the knoll. Then, as the rain increased to a deluge, Wandwyn closed his eyes and turned aside to avoid it lashing into his face. When he opened them again, he was standing on level ground and the knoll was nowhere to be seen. Soaked to the skin, he hurried home. As he ran down the slope above his farmstead, he noticed something glistening in the grass. It was a tiny, chestnut foal. It's mother was nowhere to be seen and it was so small that Wandwyn was able to lift it in his arms and carry it into the warm stable adjoining the farmhouse.

Teaching the foal to suck his fingers, Wandwyn soon had it drinking milk from a pail. Because it was such a spirited little creature, he called it Punch. Within a week Punch had grown to twice his original size and within three weeks he was eating oats and hay. He continued to grow rapidly and was soon as large as any horse in the valley. By the new year he was easily the largest and most powerful horse to be found anywhere.

Punch allowed Wandwyn to climb on his back and ride him over the moors without bridle or saddle. Soon it grew bitterly cold and the snows came. Realising he must prepare his land for seeding soon after the snows melted, Wandwyn decided to sell Punch at the Candlemass Fare on the second of February. He would surely fetch such a price that would buy him both a plough and two ordinary horses to pull it. They were making headway when a blizzard struck. Leaning forward, Wandwyn clung to the great horse's arched neck. Punch plodded on unperturbed until, a while later, he suddenly plunged up to his middle in a snowdrift. Sliding off his back, Wandwyn sank up to his armpits. Much to his surprise, he found he could move his legs freely. Pushing the snow from around his body, he found they were near the entrance to a cave, the warm air from which had melted a hollow in the snow.

Crawling through the small entrance hole, Wandwyn found himself in a cavern brightly lit with oil lamps and, there before him, was the finest plough he had ever seen along with a set of trace harness studded with gleaming brasses. By this time the warmth from the cave had melted more snow and

Punch was freed. One mighty blow from one of his rear hooves severed the rock blocking the cave entrance and Wandwyn was able to harness him to the plough, which he dragged outside as the blizzard was abating. Then, as they moved off along the way they had come, Rosina could be heard singing her haunting melody. Looking up, Wandwyn gasped at the sight of her seated on her knoll above the cavern clad this time in a white fur robe. 'Plough a furrow for me!' she called and then disappeared. Unable to find her and fearing the onset of another blizzard, Wandwyn made haste to follow homeward in the wake of Punch and the plough.

At winter's end, with Punch ploughing twice as fast as any ordinary horse, Wandwyn soon had his land ready for seeding. Deciding to ask the seed merchant if he would accept the plough in payment for seed corn, he climbed on Punch's back and set off once again across the moor. However, Punch had no intention of going to see the seed merchant, making his way instead, once again, to the blacksmith's knoll. Working away in his forge in the hillside, the blacksmith seemed not to notice their arrival and Wandwyn's attention was soon drawn to a whirring sound issuing forth from a nearby thatched hut. Dismounting and entering the hut through the open doorway, he was pleased once again to see Rosina, clad this time in a white blouse and green pinafore dress, and seated at a spinning wheel. 'If it's seed corn you're after,' she laughed, 'Don't waste your time here. Ride home and sow whatever you find in the barn.'

Wandwyn paused. 'If you say so, Rosina, then I must do as you say. But first will you not dance for me?'

Fetching a drum from a corner of the hut, Rosina bade him beat out a rhythm. Wandwyn obeyed and she began dancing, first with her eyes, then with her head and then with her hair. Then, clapping her hands high in the air, she began to step round in time to the drum beats. Her head, hands and hips blended with the breeze and her feet moved as if they were attached to the legs of the wind. Realising that his drum beats were now blending with the sound of the smith's hammer on the anvil, Wandwyn stopped beating, but Rosina continued to dance. Coming up behind him, Punch nudged him with his nose. Taking this to mean it was time to leave, Wandwyn got on his back, but the great horse decided instead to join in the dance with Rosina and pranced daintily after her round in a great circle. Meanwhile, the blacksmith, seemingly unaware of what was going on, continued to rain blows onto the hot iron, causing golden sparks to arc out all around the forge, giving the appearance of a waving ripe wheat-field.

Wandwyn became so absorbed in the ritual, which seemed to continue for a long while, he failed to notice that Rosina, the blacksmith and the forge had all disappeared until Punch finally stopped dancing when he was astonished to find they had come to a stop right in front of his barn at the farmstead. Jumping to the ground, he threw open the barn doors to find there before him a pile of seed corn. Kissing Punch on his great velvet nose, he said: 'We have our seed corn. Let's go and sow it!'

That harvest Wandwyn's farm had the highest wheat yield in the valley and his barn was filled to overflowing. The corn merchant offered him a good price, but he had no wagon with which to transport the grain. Once gain he rode Punch onto a lonely part of the moor where he presently heard a gruff voice. It was the Blacksmith sitting on a rock by the trackside. 'Why, if it isn't our young friend again!' he said. 'How would you like to come back with me to the forge for a meal?'

The hillside opened to receive them and Wandwyn found himself in a vaulted chamber arrayed all around with richly embroidered curtains. The smith bade Wandwyn be seated at a large oak table whilst Punch sat dog fashion on the floor, which intrigued Wandwyn as he'd never before seen a horse sit like that. Rosina, her hair hanging in a long pigtail down her back over a close-fitting black dress, came in and laid food before them. Her reassuring smile convinced Wandwyn that she knew he loved her, but she said nothing and, having returned a little later with hay for Punch, she retired to another room.

After the meal, the smith led Wandwyn into another vast chamber where the peasant gasped to see a brightly painted wagon with a set of harness resting on its shafts. The smith told him that the wagon would be his if he could complete two tasks. 'Come with me to the forge and I'll tell you what they are,' he said.

In the forge the smith handed Wandwyn a large iron bar telling him that he had to bend it into a U-shape using only his hands. Then, showing him a large, egg-shaped stone, he said he must lift it after he had bent the bar. He would have three attempts at each task and if he failed to accomplish either one or the other he must give Punch to the blacksmith. However if he succeeded in both tasks, the wagon would be his.

Back in the curtained chamber, Rosina had prepared a bed of sheep skins. During the night Wandwyn had a strange dream. Peering at him out of the night sky, Punch was speaking to him. 'The iron bar is the unbendable will of a closed mind and the stone is the seed of the earth's compassion.'

The following morning, having made two futile attempts to bend the iron bar, Wandwyn remembered his dream. Taking the bar to Punch, he held it under his nose, whispering for him to breathe on it. Giving vent to an obliging snort, the great horse enveloped the bar with his damp breath. Hastening to the smith and holding the bar up before him, Wandwyn bent it into a U-shape as if it were made of putty.

Nodding his appreciation, the smith reminded him that he still had to lift the stone.

Walking slowly round the hollow, Wandwyn peered inside the thatched hut where Rosina, clad in her white fur robe, was preparing her spinning wheel. 'You've no need to bother with trying to lift the stone,' she said. 'Fetch Punch and I'll guide you both out of the hollow, and I'll come with you and live with you always. It's the only way. No one has ever managed to lift the stone.'

As she continued to look at him, Wandwyn was struck by how strangely old her eyes looked and he noticed that her hair had become as white as her robe. Swallowing hard, he forced himself to say: 'No, Rosina, you know this cannot be. I must go and lift the stone.'

Having failed twice to lift the stone, Wandwyn thought hard. Walking round the hollow for a second time and coming to the hut, he walked straight inside without waiting for Rosina to bade him enter. Lying on a bed of flax, she was naked save for her flaxen hair, which flowed over her like primroses over a bank in springtime. 'Fail to lift the stone a third time and you will lose all this and Punch,' she said.

Running back to the forge, Wandwyn lifted the stone in his arms in one swift movement and carried it to the smith, who went at once and helped him harness Punch to the wagon. Then, as he prepared to drive away, he asked the smith for Rosina's hand in marriage. Indulging himself with an enigmatic smile, the smith retorted: 'Bring to me within one year from today the cup of sorrow that overflows with joy and Rosina is yours. Fail to do so and you will never be able to find this place again.'

Back at the farm, Wandwyn and Punch worked hard on the farm throughout winter and spring and well into the following summer. Wandwyn had no more helpful dreams and no one could tell him where he might find the cup of sorrow that overflowed with joy. Although he never ceased to love Rosina, he was beginning to resign himself to never seeing her again. Then, one day, as summer gave way to autumn, he was sitting with Punch under the mighty oak when the great horse suddenly rose to his feet, knocking several acorns to the ground as he did so. Gazing thoughtfully at them for several moments, Wandwyn presently bent down and picked one up.

Early the following morning, mounting Punch, he told the great horse to take him onto the moors. The year's grace was up today and there was no time to lose. Sometime later they heard singing and there was Rosina, clad in her russet coloured dress and seated upon the knoll combing her long hair. 'Father is expecting you!' she called.

'You've brought the cup, otherwise you wouldn't be here,' the smith said. 'So show it to me and explain its meaning.'

Holding up before him an acorn seated in its small cup, Wandwyn responded: 'Behold the cup of sorrow that overflows with joy. Cup and acorn together are beauty itself and the cup experiences great sorrow when the acorn leaves it to lie upon the earth, where it's destined to fulfil one of a variety of uses. Food for animals such as pigs and squirrels, it may also grow into a great tree producing many more cupped acorns. So it is that the acorn in its cup expresses the joy of producing and the sorrow of wasting, the joy of meeting and the sorrow of parting. In it joy and sorrow become one and the purpose of life is understood.'

Punch neighed and Rosina leapt into Wandwyn's arms, causing him to realise that he was now wedded to the Earth Mother herself.

THE END

DEATH

Impoverished Death,
Possessing nothing at all;
Feared by everyone;
Owned, in turn, by everything;
Possessed by the universe.

Death is the thick smoke
Rising from the fires of life;
A billowing cloud
Bringing life to a barren planet,
Raining life upon the earth;
A universal mechanism
Driving an eternal wheel
In a continuous recycling process.

Mistrusted by man
Death reigns supreme in its universe,
Emboldened by his superstitions.

Individuality
Is the obsession of man
And Death cashes in
Snatching an ephemeral embodiment
Granted by man's gullibility.

In this way
Death becomes a dark devil
Destroying the individual,
Snuffing out his light
And entombing him.

Man fears drowning in a sea of life:
He's determined to reign supreme
In his universe always,
Creating for himself a heaven,
In which personalities are perpetuated,
Unwilling to enter any life-stream,
Or to become part of any whole.

Man has enslaved Death,
Making it his tool,
His means of retribution,
Rewarding Man alone with eternity.
In turn, Death has enslaved Man,
Holding him in fear.

True death remains the whispering Death
That drives the eternal wheel
Rejuvenating the universe:
A beatifying Death
Bringing life to all
Like the melting of the snows
In an eternal springtime.

LIFE STRUGGLE

His slimy nose scenting milk,
the calf udder-nudges upwards
into me for more,

The Hessian carpet of her tongue
squirms across the floor
inside a corrugated cave
now filled with fingers
simulating teats.

Carefully, I pull her head towards
the surface of the milk inside
the silver pail and soon
she glugs and sucks the liquid warmth
of mother-sustenance.

Hers is the struggle to survive
as young grass strives
against the lash of whipping hail.

When, at last, she learns to drink
without the aid of any finger power,
adaption will have built for her
an edifice inside the puzzle
that our glibness designates as life.

THE GRUNDLY CHAIR

Booby, booby, high in the air,
See the witch in her grundly chair:
Over the aspens, down the well,
Swishity-swoosh, she weaves a spell.

Perched on her shoulder see bullfinch
Judging the distance to an inch:
He tells her how, he tells her where,
The safest place to land her chair.

This bright bullfinch, he lives with her:
Prefers she him to cat or cur:
Booby, booby, see her skip,
Picking her teeth with a paper clip.

The grundly chair has sixteen wheels;
Behind, it stores food for their meals:
Trundly, grundly, wickety-wheeze,
It rides the storm as 'twere a breeze.

The witch is merry, bright and good;
She cooks the most exciting food;
She travels round and visits all,
And folks are pleased to see her call.

Through the billowing clouds she flies
Collecting reeks for coddling pies:
She bakes them in the dead of night,
Cooling them off at morning light.

Booby, booby, high in the air,
See the witch in her grundly chair:
Over the willows, wise and tall,
She makes her way to serve us all.

*

Bodhi Day Hymn

How blessed is the Bodhi Tree
That gave the Buddha shade;
More blessed by far are those who see
That here the Path was laid.

No more need any doubt the way
To cause all pain to cease;
Lord Buddha shows us on this day
The light of perfect peace.

Of pain there seems to be no end,
Desire is never still;
Remove the cause, the truth defend
By eight controls of will.

If gods and demons all disdain
The power of Buddhahood,
May we forever know the gain
When Mind is understood.

Rejoice in Buddha then this day
That all the world may share
His joyous love, the only way
That all may truly care.

He brings to us in every word
Compassionate release;
He is our All-Enlightened Lord,
Our Mighty Prince of Peace.

How blessed is the Bodhi Tree
That gave the Buddha shade;
More blest by far are those who see
That here the Path was laid.

*

OLD OCTOPUS

Old Octopus the tree has eight gnarled arms
Holding up a lacelike head of ale,
In which these forty rooks dip deep their beaks
And, looking up, proclaim his silken worth.

Bubbling loose as foam blown from the sea,
His frothy hair lifts, drifting free to touch
The silken face of Chinese tapestries
To flux their rugged scenes with dancing plumes.

Just where it levels with the singing earth
His trunk is footed like an elephant,
With four great toes protruding to the west
In opposition to his windswept head.

Old Octopus has stood fast in this place
Two hundred years. Through all that time his leaves
Have fed him from the skies and underfoot,
His roots have drunk his health and held him firm.

This place, the hills, the sea, the sky are his;
His stretching arms proclaim his templedom;
His congregations are the rooks who voice
His prayer-less power beyond the bonds of time.

LIGHT VERSE AND WORSE

RED KNICKERS

I've seen fair beauties lying under silken sheets;
I've seen them walking neatly down the city streets;
I've seen them lying naked on a sunny beach
With golden hair and bottoms rounded like a peach:
>But although they're all so lovely,
>As lovely as can be,
>I'd rather have my Jenny
>In red knickers on my knee.

I've seen some lovely nurses walking on the wards
And one a pretty peeress in the House of Lords;
I've seen a girls suspenders when the wind was strong
And cuddled buxom beauties when the night was long:
>But although they're all so lovely,
>As lovely as can be,
>I'd rather have my Jenny
>In red knickers on my knee.

I've sat and watched the mermaids combing out their locks;
I've kissed some merry milkmaids in their linen smocks;
I've danced a jig with Mary on the village green,
As handsome girl as any you have ever seen:
>But although they're all so lovely,
>As lovely as can be,
>I'd rather have my Jenny
>In red knickers on my knee.

GUSTAVUS LING

There was an old fellow called Gustavus Ling
Who couldn't remember the name of a thing;
He never could tell if a flag was unfurled
Or whether a cabbage was crinkled or curled.
      Hoorah for old Gustavus, Gustavus Ling
      Who could never remember the name of a thing.

Inhaler, adhesive and rodenticide
Are names which he hated and couldn't abide;
Nose-easer, rat-killer and strong sticky stuff
Are terms which he used when the going got tough.
      Hoorah for old Gustavus, Gustavus Ling
      Who could never remember the name of a thing.

Yarn weaver, cold cleaver, that juice saving thing,
Soil heaver, wood reaver and thigamy jing:
He made up his own names as he went along;
He couldn't remember, but never went wrong.
      Hoorah for old Gustavus, Gustavus Ling
      Who could never remember the name of a thing.

They taught him painstakingly right from a boy
To call things by names such as *engine* and *toy*.
He was happy with *horse*, with *tumbrel* and *bread*.
Internal dynamics just filled him with dread.
      Hoorah for old Gustavus, Gustavus Ling
      Who could never remember the name of a thing.

They tried to confuse him with many fine words;
He paid no attention and talked to the birds;
Gustavus Ling never wanted a caption;
When lost for a name, he just shouted: CONTRAPTION.
> Hoorah for old Gustavus, Gustavus Ling
> Who could never remember the name of a thing.

THE SPIDER

Here behind the dusty curtain rail,
Sitting silently upon a nail,
Concealed, contented in her silken home,
The wary spider looks into the room
Seeing everything that goes on there
Whether it be foolish, foul or fair,
Whether it be noble, false or true,
Combing hair or tying up a shoe.
Providing no one dusts behind the rail
She knows that she will never starve or fail:
Except, of course, if some one in a pique
To slaughter all the flies should truly seek;
Or, giving way to creepy-crawly fears,
Scream out blue murder in her tiny ears:
Like once when sweet and twenty, dainty Meg
Feared that a spider would run up her leg.
She never did of course: indeed 'twas worse
(Surprising that Meg did not cry or curse)
When Charlie went where spider mustn't go
And did far worse than she could ever do.
She loves to spin her web within this house
Where no one screams at sight of squeaking mouse,
Or wants to kill all living things in sight
Because they fear they'll bite them in the night.
She knows it's all a pack of nasty lies
That makes folk hate her worse than filthy flies:
Both she and flies they squirt with noxious killer
And try to wall her up with plastic filler;
But she knows she's safe from all such things

Living with a kindly dame who sings
And never sweeps the cobwebs from the doors
Or worries when mice run across the flowers:
She never has a fly within her house
And keeps a cat to master Mister Mouse.
Oh yes, the flies fly in for sure, that's true,
But Missus Spider makes them into stew.
She never fails to please all those who trust
The web of life and do not fear the dust,
 Which settles there upon the curtain rail:
They know her industry will never fail:
Her splendid artistry fits into it,
As anyone who has the time to sit
And watch her labours will indeed confirm,
As once before the Bruce she did a term
Of patient and spruce spinning in a cave,
Which caused that king to cease lament and shave,
And go and win a dozen battles more,
Despite the fact his noble feet were sore.
So when all things at work are going wrong,
Just lift your voice and sing this merry song:
The spider spins and weaves at home for me;
She guards my house and keeps it insect free.

THE PEST

Could you tell me. I wonder, my dearest wee pest
Why it is that you live in the earth with the rest,
Why you dance with all creatures in pleasant accord
And then skewer them all on the point of your sword?

Dear sir, you must realise, I have to be strong;
In my youth I was gentle and never did wrong;
In the joy of my service I tried for the best,
But discovered my plans would not work with the rest.

They never did realise I needed a niche
For the earth to continue both fertile and rich;
So they shouted in panic: 'Get rid of this pest!'
And they poisoned me off in the earth with the rest.

I divided up quickly and left me a part
To continue in business and make a new start,
Then I fed on the poison and grew big and strong
And that's why I'm able to sing you this song.

MAGGIE'S DUMPLINGS

You should have seen our Maggie's
Dumplings bouncing like a ball;
There weren't a man in Suffolk
Could ha' mastered them at all:
She baked them in her oven
At the falling of the dew
And boiled them in the morning
In a pot of cabbage stew.

She gave them to her Johnny
When he came home from his work:
He said: 'Lord love us Maggie,
They're a twisting up me fork!'
They twined around his elbows
Like the squirming of a snake;
Poor Johnny ran into the woods
 And jumped into a lake.

Our Maggie cried: 'Oh Johnny,
'What's the matter with you mate?'
And offered him her dumplings
Served on a silver plate:
 'Hang onto these, me darling
And I'll pull you to the shore'
But Johnny cried: 'No thank you gal,
I've tried that lark afore!'

The dumplings fell into the depths
And mangled up the tide;
Brave Johnny swam and cried: 'Thank God!'
And reached the other side.
He lifted up his legs and ran
And holed up at his ma's;
He got divorced and wed young Jill
A girl who wore no bras.

There was this man from Norfolk
Who contrived to eat a lot:
He said he'd chewed his mother's
When a baby in his cot:
He chewed on one of Maggie's
From the evening to the dawn,
When she rolled him through the window
And bounced him on the lawn.

Then came Big Pete from Yorkshire
With a belly like a bull:
He stuck a dumpling in his teeth
And gave a mighty pull.
He pulled until his arm was straight:
His fingers then let go.
You should have seen how he flew back
To land in Maggie's loo!

Saint Mary's Church was crumbling fast
From all the stress and strain;
Its undermined foundations
Were washing down the drain:

'If we don't find some money,'
Said the rector in distress,
'This church will fall by Eastertide
And that is not a guess.'

'Quick! Use our Maggie's dumplings.'
Someone shouted from the back,
'She keeps them in her cycle shed
'And sells them by the sack.'
So they stayed the church with dumplings
In sacks beneath its walls,
Causing them to oscillate
Like a million rubber balls.

The rector lurched along the aisle
And bounced from side to side;
He looked as green as if he'd been
A sailing through the tide:
The choir twisted in their shoes
And shook their trembling feet;
They rocked and rolled like dumplings
To the time of Maggie's beat.

ON SHARPENING KNIVES

Have any of you met the bore who knows
It all and takes great trouble as he shows
The keenest way to sharpen up your knife
Upon a stone he's had there all his life?

I use to sharpen mine upon a hone
Until, one day, he called out: 'Use my stone!
'You'll never get an edge upon it thus.'
I gave in to his whim to save a fuss.

'First smear across the stone,' he said, 'Some oil;
'But not too much in case you tend to spoil
'The rhythmic action of your circling thrust
'And cause the end to slip up through your bust.'

I rubbed my knife upon the stone in dread,
And sure enough: 'That's not the way,' he said:
He took it from my hand and felt he blade:
'With this you couldn't dig out marmalade!'

'Correct the angle of your knife in place,
'Unless you want its edge to be like lace;
'Be careful not to hold the tool too straight,
'And stroke towards you at a gentle rate.'

He tested out the edge upon his thumb
And deftly flicked the blade and said: 'Ah, hum!
'This knife will cut up any hair you like,
'Or slice the belly of a stubborn pike.'

I took the knife and cut a piece of twine.
'I'd not do that if the knife were mine,'
He said. 'You've taken off the edge again
'And all my careful sharpening 's in vain.'

I seized the knife and ran back to the hone
And polished up the knife until it shone;
I called my best friend in to have a look
And showed her how to do it by the book.

'This is the way I always sharpen mine,'
I said. 'And as it pleases me, that's fine.
'You twist it thus and rub it on the side,
'Then bring it back and gently let it slide.'

'No! No!' she cried, 'You mustn't do it so;
'I always sharpen mine upon my shoe:
'To sharpen it like that will never last;
'They never did it that way in the past.'

'Not even when they had no shoes to wear?'
I asked. 'Or perhaps they never had to care
When flint knives were the order of the day
And everyone used them to kill their prey.

My friend was not amused, to say the least.
'You do not use this knife to kill a beast,'
She said. 'Indeed to sharpen it's an art,
'And if you don't believe me, we must part.'

So, if you want your friendships to endure,
Just let your knives go blunt, and that's for sure;
For once you let him in, the sharpening bore
Will rob you of your peace forevermore.

(End of Light Verse and Worse)

WOMAN

Woman is hair blowing in the wind
And rippling laughter
Dancing on the village green.
Woman is a girl skipping over the molehills
And swinging on a branch
Kicking her legs and showing her knickers.
Woman is the warmth of a smile
Soothing away cares.
She pierces pain like a lightening shaft
And shatters it into a thousand pieces.
Woman is Earth Goddess,
The essence of life feeding the world
With love and laughter.
When she loses all of these
The woman dies in her.

MESSAGES

Like waves lip-lapping on the lochan shore,
The flop of beaten egg
In a rock embattled basin,
Prayer flags fly beside the almond trees
Out across the lake,
Flapping like the flap of whale flippers,
Slapping the air like a snorting horse
Praying to the stars.

Like the fluttering bird upon the window pane,
Like fear before the fight,
Like the bursting heart before the tryst,
The flags wave out their messages,
Lapping at the scented air.

Fear is the flutter of flags;
Joy is the flutter of flags;
Prayer is flags fluttering,
Thoughts smacking in the breeze
Like waves lip-lapping on the lochan shore.

VALKYRIE

Who asks for silence when the thunder sounds,
When beating hooves foretell the massacre
Of all who flee before the flailing sword
Cut down in flight before their burning homes?
Twisting, terror struck, they turn and fall
Before the Battle Maidens' scourging ride,
Cut down because they flee and do not stand,
Cut down because they long for silence
When the thunder sounds.

Who asks for silence when the drum beat rolls
Beside this Battle Maiden's leaping horse,
Her horse that leaps and leaves behind the dead
That lie beneath the drum beats on the plain?
Silent they lie slaughtered on the grass
Like fresh baked bannocks on a baker's bench
Awaiting purchase by the passers by.
Heedless of the plunging horses' hooves
Silent now, they rest.

Who asks for silence when the jackal howls?
Beside the round and radiating baps
Bespattering the plain before the tents,
These dead who never learnt, nor cared to learn,
The message of the thunder's crashing call,
And now can never hear the voice that warns
Them of the Battle Maiden's bloody sword
Emboldened by hyenas' mocking calls
As vultures come to rest.

MOTHER GODDESS

Earth-dark and dutiful,
Her body pierced by a sharp sword,
Her blood blending with the flow of her hair
And staining the grass red,
The goddess lies raped on the green sward:
Raped by greed and dying slowly
Beneath the laughter of the lone leaf's lingering fall.

Her life laughing out of her,
She refuses to die,
Herself lingering,
Floating on the fall of the leaf,
Her every breath blazing a hot trail to the heart of God
And growing stronger.

Sizzling under the hot thrust, God combines with Man.
They struggle to lift the sword from her body,
Seeking its stroke to sweep the leaf from the air
And smother their guilt.
Knowing they have violated and rejected her
They fear her continuous dying will reconcile the opposites
And fix the leaf forever in the air.

Life springing from the dark earth
Grows beautiful in the flow of her blood,
Mocking the rapacity of Man
And revealing God's irrelevance.
The smile on her dying lips swells
And gushes into laughing continuity.

THE MIND'S EYE BELL

Beneath the beams in godless quietude
Angels fly within the old church roof,
Brushing with their wings the oaken shields
Supporting, in decay, decrepitude.

Deathless peace pervades their sacred realm
Pushing mindfulness to slumberland,
Singing softly to the prayerful sage,
Who sits unmindful of their swinging helm.

Communicating with his deity
Visions roll across his mistful mind
Teaching him some secret mysteries:
Some powerful perks increasing piety.

Secure within this soothing solitude,
Heedless of the flying angel host,
Wisdom-wreathed, unseeing sits the sage
Heedless of crying and solicitude.

Hymns from the worshippers of days gone by
Here are trapped within this time-filled sphere:
Smiling melodies are on the move;
As angels borne on tuneful wings they fly.

It is this pensive child alone can tell,
Standing here in silent wonderment,
The secrets of the oaken beams above:
He needs no god to ring his mind's eye bell.

WEREWOLF

Wolf howls are communication:
Man howls are frustration and despair.
So Man despises Wolf and kills him,
Thinking to stop his own whining,
To still his own complaining,
And restore his fortunes.

Man envies Wolf:
So he makes himself Werewolf.
He howls like a wolf;
But he doesn't comprehend:
His howl is still a complaint.

Man becomes more frustrated than ever:
He kills now because he's afraid,
No longer because he's hungry.
He kills Wolf because he fears him:
He fears himself in the wolf;
He fears the wolf in himself:
So he tells lies about Wolf to get him hated,
Because he fears to hate himself.
But Wolf has no hatred:
He kills merely to survive.

THE SMILE

I was born beneath an oak tree
In the whispering of the breeze:
I was born beneath an oak tree
As the sun shone through the trees.

I was born at the break of day
Where flies the grey-winged bat:
I was born at the dawn of time
Where Gotama Buddha sat.

I was born in the beginning
And also at the end;
I was born in the beginning
With a lifetime for my friend.

My mother was the bride of day;
Her body was the night:
Her bright blue eyes shone out like stars
Without the aid of light.

She dressed me in the dew of dawn
Where glossy spider weaves:
She fed me with the milk of truth
And laid me in the leaves.

Ten thousand birds sang out with joy;
All love was in that place:
Gotama Buddha smiled a smile:
I laughed into his face.

ART HORSE

Art is this white horse
Painted on a blue background,
His black harness
Enhancing the beauty of his flanks,
His arched neck
Emphasising the power of his legs.

Such art captures his reality
In the stroke of a moment,
Revealing the true horse
And glossing over nothing.

Conversely,
This pretty picture
Submerges the horse
In a sea of sentiment,
Concealing his reality
Like a mocking waxwork
Or a jerry-built house.

It's better
To create nothing more
Than a bold brush stroke
Than to earn praise
For painstaking plurality.

ART HORSE PROCLAIMS HIMSELF

I am Art Horse:
Mind projected on a moving canvass:
The embodiment of man's search
For the secrets of the universe.

I am Beauty:
Form envisaged on a changing background:
The embodiment of truth,
Revealing the secrets of the universe.

I am Function:
The mind form of the universe
Living in the mind of Art Horse,
Who is the embodiment of beauty and its function.

THE OLD LANE

Drifting into the distance
And merging silently
With the cloudy green elm tops,
The old lane snaked its way
Passed the abode of Art Horse
In a sophisticated profusion
Of rambling entanglement,
Its high hedges,
Honeysuckle entwined and enticingly scented,
Penetrated by persistent owl hoots
In the cool of the evening.

Art Horse stirred,
Wondering at the tale it had to tell.
'Artist, paint the poetry of the lane
'And let the truth be told,' he said.

Dipping his brush,
The artist boldly stroked his canvass,
Painting blazing colours
Splashed in vivid strokes like owl hoots
Shooting through the night
And cutting holes in the hedges
To open up a scene
That few desired to see
Or think about
He painted the life of man
As the beat of an owl's wing
Silently brushing the night:

Necessity as the owl's hunger;
Pain as the broken back of a mouse
Seized in the owl's talons;
The judgement of right and wrong
As the conflict between pain and necessity;
Survival as the battle for light
In the heaving hedgerow;
As the struggle of the worker
On the endless production line,
Unnoticed like the passing beat of an owl's wing,
Surviving only in its perception
Of the bright eye piercing the solid night.
Art Horse saw and said:
'You've painted well:
'Tomorrow I will walk the path
'And know myself the truth you paint.'

ART HORSE WALKS IN THE WOODS

Swaying to the chant of harness chains
Art Horse paced along the woodland ways
Snorting mists among the bursting buds
To blend his breath in chorus with the birds,
Whose songs flew round about to rub the rust
Forever from the tinkling breeching chains,
Their music mixing to control in time
The chariots upon the wheel of life.

On seeing him the boy stood still and smiled.
'Art Horse, haul me here this loaded cart of logs
'To fuel the fires of my desire,' he said,
'For I have need to make my mark on life.'

'If you should burn these logs upon your fire,
'How would the fire continue when they're burned?'

'More logs must then be carried to the blaze.'

'Indeed, and then more still until the fire
Would increase even more in its desire
Until no forest would be left at all:
And should you burn the whole wide world around
Unabated still desire would thrive:
Is this the way to make your mark on life?'

The boy stood by the horse's velvet nose
And felt it fondly soft against his face.
'Within these woods, Art Horse,' he said, 'There lives

'A small, voracious beast called Ranny Shrew
Who, driven by the fire of his desires,
Steers fast persistently through leafy seas,
A sharp-fanged shark in search of sustenance,
A terror to his chitin-coated prey,
Which lurks in earthy, spore-infested dens
Beneath the whispering waves of dark decay,
Themselves possessing predatory power
And governed by desire as with the shrew,
This same desire that drives them all to mate
In order to perpetuate their race:
Without desire how can the wheel rotate,
And how can shrews or any life survive?'

Art Horse shook his mane and twitched his silky ears.
'Come harness me to pull the cart and tell
Me how its wheels turn round and move along.'

The boy obeyed Art Horse and told him this:
'The axle holds the wheels and they rotate
'Through hubs and spokes that turn the felloes
'Holding firm the iron tyres on the rim.'

'Yes, indeed,' said Art Horse patiently,
'The turning of a wheel is like a web
'In which each part depends upon the other
'And not one part alone controls the whole.
'The shrew is but a spoke within the wheel
'And has no power to stop its constant turning
'As you have now, your hand upon the reins.
'I pull the cart and cause the wheels to turn,

'But only on a signal through the reins;
'And so it is, you see, you have the power
'To stop the racing wheel of fond desire
'Or race it fast and crush the fragile web.

'On the one hand you must learn to curb
'The fires of your desire and thus preserve
'The web of life intact upon the wheel.
'But then again you need to break the wheel
'That you may free yourself beyond the bonds
'Of time's indifference. A strand within
'The web, the ranny thrives from day to day
'Bound to the ever turning wheel of fate:
'So leave him there and let him turn in peace
'And through your understanding of his place,
'Control the reins and stop the turning wheel
'In your own mind and tread the path of truth.'

The boy loaded up the cart with logs
And drove with Art Horse to his forest home,
And there he stabled him in golden straw
And fed him oats and sweetly scented hay.
He used the logs to light a fire for warmth
And meditated on the things he'd learned.

ART BIRTH

Hoisting heavenward on rook-black hooves,
Art Horse strives to climb the rungs of dusk
And, launching from the topmost stave,
Untrammelled flies, a bright-winged Pegasus,
Who, striking sparks from flecks of gritty night,
Equips the mind, illuminating all
Its crevices until the truth is found.

Art Horse, white hot wind horse, onward strikes
To blaze his sparkling trail to teach the mind
To paint the stars as flowers among the trees
Within the realm of gritty, shade-filled night.

Fire has many shapes
As, born within the blazing heat of stars,
It lives to agonise the birth of art
Within the mind, inside its shady groves,
In which its secrets wander wistfully
Endeavouring to master everything
And shaping art in all its many forms.
Until it casts them out, as meteors
That fly with Art Horse out beyond the stars.

ERIC and EMMA

Emily wondered about other women. Friends were all very well, but could they always be trusted? Would they, maybe, become too friendly with one's very own man? Although she wasn't attracted to any of her friends' husbands, she might one day find a new friend whose husband she would find irresistible. And what if he fell in love with her at first sight? This did happen. It had happened to her – across the dance floor, and he'd now been her husband for thirty years. Theirs was a happy marriage, but love wasn't limited and, although she was now over fifty, what was to stop her falling in love with a second man?

In some societies, the Inuit for instance, it had been the custom for a woman to have more than one husband. Polyandry she believed they called it. This meant that a husband could always be left at home to protect the wife when the other husbands were away on long hunting trips. Sadly, this had also meant that too many girl babies were seen as a handicap, resulting in some of them being put out on the ice to freeze quickly to death. But she wasn't an Inuit and she didn't want any more babies. Anyway, she was too old. But another man was different. She tried to picture how she would like him to be.

First, she gave him a name: Eric. It had a Viking ring to it: Eric the Red and all that; and she had always been attracted to northern men: Fred was from Northumberland. However, she didn't fancy being abducted by Vikings, always preferring creative men with interesting minds. Yes, that was it, she would like Eric to be a poet, a writer, an artist, a musician. But she didn't move in those circles. Besides, she'd heard that artistic people were temperamental. Fred was easy-going and practical and she liked that. But, then again, not twice over. She fancied retaining Fred as her anchor with a passionate, temperamental paramour hidden away for weekend days when Fred was away at the football match. That was their one disagreement. She hated football and that's why they had two television sets.

It was the Friday night match that did it. It was a cup match and Fred simply couldn't miss it, not even to go dancing with Emily. Undeterred, she went on her own. An accomplished ballroom dancer, she was never without a partner. In particular, a tall, well-figured young man, with bright eyes and a winsome smile, showed interest in her. So much so, in fact, that she was soon dancing with no one else. It was some time since she had danced with such an adept partner.

'We should do this more often,' he said. 'The young women could learn an awful lot from you. Don't tell me, you must be a dancing tutor?'

Emily shook her head. 'You flatter me. But tell me what you do. I could just as easily say the same about you.'

'And you'd be wrong. I'm a dress designer. That's to say, I design clothes with ladies' underwear as my speciality. Much of my work is for a well known retailer. You may have heard of me under my professional name. My real name's Nathaniel; but everyone calls me "Nat"…' He paused as if expecting a response.

Emily obliged. 'But what're you doing here? I mean, I'm here often…'

'And you've never seen me? Well, that's easily explained. This is my first visit. We're doing a shoot down on the beach. The long expanse of sand's just right for showing off my latest designs in the sunlight.'

'I expect you're often away from home.'

'Sometimes; but I work a lot at weekends to suit those of our models who are part time. That's why I've never married. I admit to girl friends, but no marriage. But look… with a figure like yours you could model clothes for… for…'

'For the older woman?' Emily prompted with a wry smile.

Nat nodded. 'Something like that. I take it you're free at weekends?'

Emily's heart leapt. 'I'll do it,' she said.

'It'll mean posing around in a state of undress most of the time, even occasionally with suspenders and that kind of thing,' Nat warned.

Emily giggled. 'I'd like that,' she said. 'Even though I already have a good job.'

'Then weekends should suit you just fine.' He mentioned the name of a place about twenty miles away. 'You have a car?'

Emily nodded. 'I shop there, mostly on Saturdays, sometimes Sundays. But there's just one other thing: do you mind if I call you Eric?'

Nat liked that. 'And you'll be Emma. That's your professional name,' he laughed.

So it was that, whilst Fred watched the creative artistry of his favourite strip kicking a ball around, Emily had a ball and got a kick out of stripping off as Emma for her favourite creative artist Eric.

THE END

The Nettle

The articulate nettle
Persists at various levels,
Dripping lanterns from his upper storeys
Like a well lit pagoda.

The first guest in a fire-hollowed hospice,
He rewards its hospitality
By turning it into a temple
Announced by a thousand pagodas.

He never goes out of his way
To make conversation,
But when he is addressed,
He replies to suite the occasion.

Feared most for his penetrating comment,
He is devious underground,
Where his true power is to be found
In undercover activity.

Hefty beings moving at a superficial level
Fail to appreciate the life style of the nettle;
Only the not so obvious, softly bothersome moth
Moves unsigned in the flame of his life force.

About the Author

For most of his life Anthony Weedon has lived in remote rural places away from towns and cities. He was an Anglican priest for twenty one years, fifteen of them in Ireland, but left Christianity in 1975 and led a very happy life working first in horticulture and then as a management services officer, retiring from that job to live in Lincolnshire with his wife Jenny, after which he began to write books, two of which, The Sisterhood and Artichokes with Alice, have been published by Authorhouse. Tony's and Jenny's long interest in both Buddhism and Humanism is reflected in much of what he writes.